I0719676

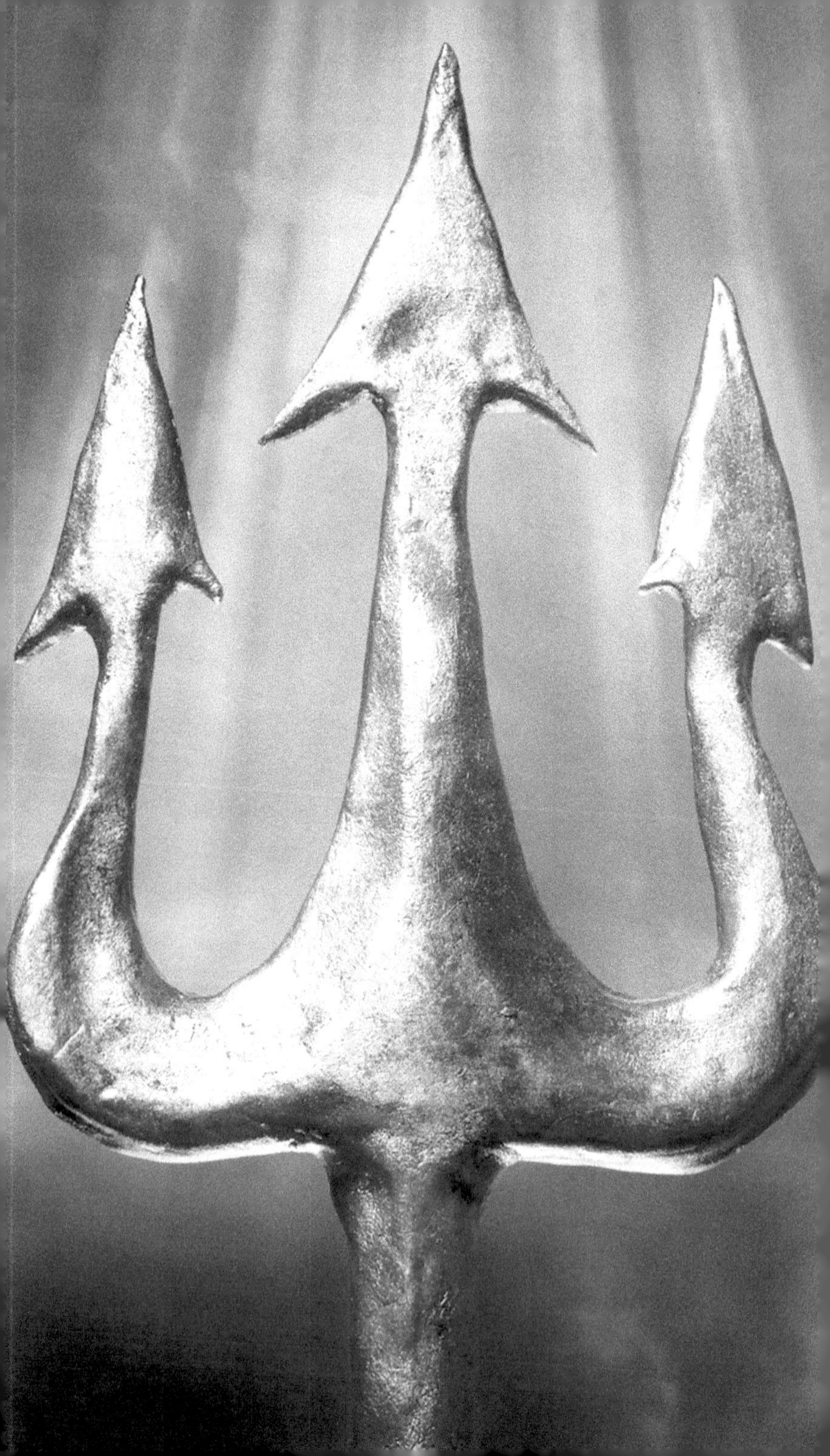

TRIDENT SECURITY
Field Manual

SAMANTHA COLE

AUTHOR'S NOTE

The story within these pages is completely fictional but the concepts of BDSM are real. If you do choose to participate in the BDSM lifestyle, please research it carefully and take all precautions to protect yourself. Fiction is based on real life but real life is *not* based on fiction. Remember—Safe, Sane and Consensual!

Any information regarding persons or places has been used with creative literary license so there may be discrepancies between fiction and reality. The missions and personal qualities of members of the military and law enforcement within have been created to enhance the story and, again, may be exaggerated and not coincide with reality.

The author has full respect for the members of the United States military and the varied members of law enforcement and thanks them for their continuing service to making this country as safe and free as possible.

INTRODUCTION

The Trident Security Field Manual: Standard Operating Procedures for FNGs (f*cking new guys—and anyone else who wants to read it) is a fun compilation of extras for fans of the TS series and its spinoffs. Some of the sections may include spoilers for books released prior to November 1, 2018, so please use caution if you haven't caught up on everyone's stories.

The Who's Who and the History of Trident Security and The Covenant are available at the front of most of the Trident Security books. However, additional information has been added for the field manual. Four of the five short stories had been previously published on www.samanthacolebook s.com, but are no longer available on the website. The fifth short story—a preview of Jenn and Doug's story—has never been released.

Also included are a list of Character Profiles for those who have found their happy-ever-afters in already released books in the original TS series and the Doms of The

Covenant series, a Q&A featuring them and several characters from the Omega Team, and the family trees of the Sexy Six-Pack. I hope you enjoy all the extras that went into this fun project. As more stories and characters are added to the TS series and its spinoffs, future volumes of this book will be published with updates.

Thanks for loving my characters and asking for more of their stories. It means the world to me.

Love,

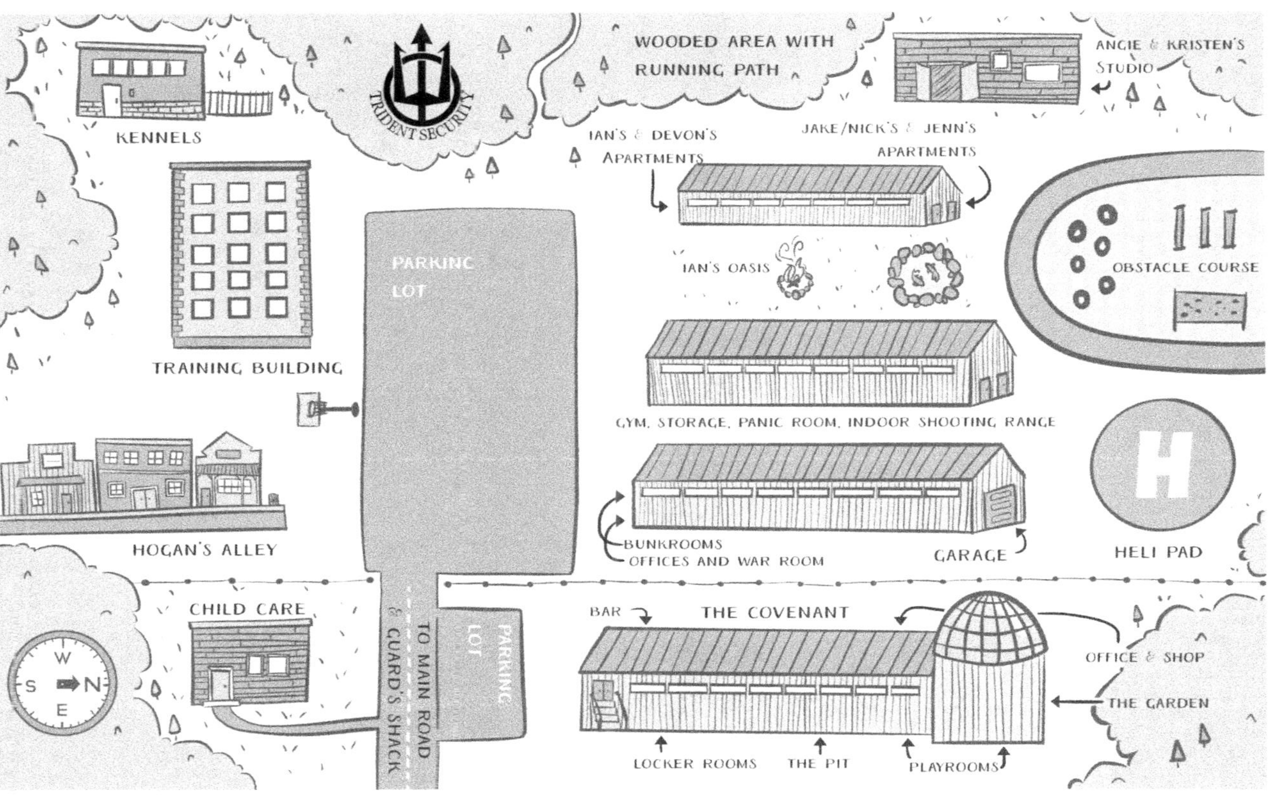

KENNELS
TRIDENT SECURITY
WOODED AREA WITH RUNNING PATH
ANGIE & KRISTEN'S STUDIO
IAN'S & DEVON'S APARTMENTS
JAKE/NICK'S & JENN'S APARTMENTS
TRAINING BUILDING
IAN'S OASIS
OBSTACLE COURSE
GYM, STORAGE, PANIC ROOM, INDOOR SHOOTING RANGE
HOGAN'S ALLEY
BUNKROOMS OFFICES AND WAR ROOM
GARAGE
HELI PAD
PARKING LOT
CHILD CARE
W
N
S
E
TO MAIN ROAD & GUARD'S SHACK
PARKING LOT
BAR
THE COVENANT
OFFICE & SHOP
THE GARDEN
LOCKER ROOMS
THE PIT
PLAYROOMS

PART ONE
WHO'S WHO AND
THE HISTORY OF
TRIDENT SECURITY
AND THE COVENANT

***While not every character is in every book, these have the most mentions throughout the series. This guide will help keep readers straight about who's who (through November 1, 2018)

Trident Security (TS) is a private investigative and military agency co-owned by Ian and Devon Sawyer. With governmental and civilian contracts, the company started when the brothers and a few of their teammates from SEAL Team Four retired to the private sector. The original six-man team is referred to as the Sexy Six-Pack, as they were dubbed by Kristen Sawyer, née Anders, or the Alpha Team. Those men and the youngest Sawyer brother, Nick Donovan, are now co-owners of the company. Trident has since expanded, and former military and law enforcement members have been added to the staff. The company is located on a guarded compound that formerly belonged to an import/export company covering a drug trafficking operation in Tampa, Florida. Three warehouses on the property were converted into large apartments, the TS offices, a gym, and bunkrooms. There is also an obstacle course, a Main Street shooting gallery, a helicopter pad, K9 kennels, a gutted, four-story building with moveable interior walls, and more features necessary for training and missions.

In addition to the security business, there is a fourth warehouse that now houses an elite BDSM club, co-owned by Devon, Ian, and their cousin, Mitch Sawyer, who is the manager. Much time and money has gone into making The Covenant the most sought-after membership in the Tampa/St. Petersburg area and beyond. Members are thoroughly vetted before being granted access to the elegant club.

Over forty Doms have been appointed Dungeon Masters (DMs), and they rotate two or three shifts each throughout the month. At least four DMs are always on duty at various posts in the pit, playrooms, and the new garden, with an additional one roaming around. Their job is to ensure the safety of all the submissives in the club. They step in if a sub uses their safeword and the Dom in the scene doesn't hear or heed it, and ensure the equipment used in scenes isn't harming the subs.

The Covenant's security team members take care of everything that isn't scene-related and provide safety for everyone. They're, essentially, the bouncers. With the recent addition of the garden and more private themed rooms, the owners have expanded their limit to 350 members. The fire marshal had approved them for 500 when the warehouse-turned-kink club first opened, but the cousins had intentionally kept that number down to maintain their elite status. With more room, they are increasing the membership to 500, still under the new maximum occupancy of 720.

The apartments in the warehouse on the opposite end of the property from the club belong to Ian and Angie, Devon and Kristen, Jake and Nick, and Jenn. Between that building and the one that houses the gym is a grassy backyard Angie designed for her husband's birthday, calling it Ian's Oasis. It features an outdoor kitchen, a large-scale barbecue, a fire pit, a koi pond with a small waterfall, and several seating areas. A misting system keeps the area cool in the hot Florida summers. On the other side of the apartment building is a small cottage built for Kristen and Angie to work in while having room for their children to play and sleep.

Between Trident Security and The Covenant, there's plenty of romance, suspense, and steamy encounters. Come meet the Sexy Six-Pack, their friends, family, and teammates.

The Sexy Six-Pack (Alpha Team) and Their Significant Others

- Ian "Boss-man" Sawyer: Devon and Nick's brother; retired Navy SEAL; co-owner of Trident Security and The Covenant; husband/Dom of Angelina.

- Devon "Devil Dog" Sawyer: Ian and Nick's brother; retired Navy SEAL; co-owner of Trident Security and The Covenant; husband/Dom of Kristen; father of John Devon "JD."
- Ben "Boomer" Michaelson: retired Navy SEAL; explosives and ordnance specialist; co-owner of Trident Security; husband/Dom of Katerina; son of Rick and Eileen.
- Jake "Reverend" Donovan: retired Navy SEAL; temporarily assigned to run the West Coast team; sniper; co-owner of Trident Security; husband/Dom of Nick; brother of Mike; Whip Master at The Covenant.
- Brody "Egghead" Evans: retired Navy SEAL; computer specialist; co-owner of Trident Security; husband/Dom of Fancy.
- Marco "Polo" DeAngelis: retired Navy SEAL; communications specialist and backup helicopter pilot; husband/Dom of Harper; father to Mara.
- Nick "Junior" Donovan, née Sawyer: Ian and Devon's younger brother; retired Navy SEAL; current operative and co-owner of Trident Security; husband/submissive of Jake Donovan.
- Kristen "Ninja-girl" Sawyer, née Anders: NYT and USA Today Bestselling Author of romance/suspense novels; wife/submissive of Devon; mother of "JD."
- Angelina "Angie/Angel" Sawyer, née Beckett: graphic artist; wife/submissive of Ian.

- Katerina "Kat" Michaelson, née Maier: dog trainer for law enforcement and private agencies; wife/submissive of Boomer.
- Millicent "Harper" DeAngelis, née Williams: lawyer; wife/submissive of Marco; mother of Mara.
- Francine "Fancy" Maguire, née Bayles-McGuire: baker and owner of Fancy's Creations; wife/submissive of Brody.

Extended Family, Friends, and Associates of the Sexy Six-Pack

- Mitch Sawyer: Cousin of Ian, Devon, and Nick; co-owner/manager of The Covenant, Dom of Tyler and Tori.
- T. Carter: US spy and assassin; works for covert US government agency Deimos; Dom of Jordyn.
- Jordyn Alvarez: US spy and assassin; member of covert US government agency Deimos; submissive of Carter.
- Tyler Ellis: Stockbroker; lifestyle switch; Dom of Tori; submissive of Mitch.
- Tori Freyja: K9 trainer for veterans in need of assistance/service dogs; submissive of Mitch and Tyler.
- Parker Christiansen: owner of New Horizons Construction; husband/Dom of Shelby; adoptive father of Franco and Victor.

- Shelby Christiansen, née Whitman: stay-at-home mom; two-time cancer survivor; wife/submissive of Parker; adoptive mother of Franco and Victor.
- Curt "Elmer" Bannerman: retired Navy SEAL; owner of Halo Customs, a motorcycle repair and detail shop; husband of Dana; father of Erica (born three years after their story); stepfather of Ryan, Taylor, Justin, and Amanda. Lives in Iowa.
- Dana Prichard-Bannerman: teacher; widow of retired SEAL Eric Prichard; wife of Curt; mother of Ryan, Taylor, Justin, Amanda, and Erica. Lives in Iowa.
- Jenn "Baby-girl" Mullins: college student; goddaughter of Ian; "niece" of Devon, Brody, Jake, Boomer, and Marco; father was a Navy SEAL; parents murdered. Student at University of Tampa.
- Mike Donovan: owner of the Irish pub, Donovan's; brother of Jake, submissive/significant other of Charlotte.
- Charlotte "Mistress China" Roth: Parole officer; Domme/significant other of Mike; Whip Master at The Covenant.
- Travis "Tiny" Daultry: former professional football player; head of security at The Covenant and Trident compound; occasional bodyguard for TS.
- Doug "Bullseye" Henderson: retired Marine; head of the Personal Protection Division of TS.

- Rick and Eileen Michaelson: Boomer's parents; guardians of Alyssa. Rick is a retired Navy SEAL.
- Charles "Chuck" and Marie Sawyer: Ian, Devon, and Nick's parents. Charles is a self-made real estate billionaire. Marie is a plastic surgeon involved with Project Smile. Third son, John, died at seventeen of alcohol poisoning.
- Dr. Roxanne and Kayla London: pediatrician and social worker, respectively. Domme and submissive, respectively. Mistress Roxy is a Whip Master at The Covenant.
- Grayson and Remington Mann: fraternal twins; owners of Black Diamond Records; Doms/fiancés of Abigail; members of The Covenant.
- Abigail "Abby" Turner: personal assistant at Black Diamond Records; submissive/fiancée of Gray and Remi.
- Chase Dixon: retired Marine Raider; owner of Blackhawk Security; associate of TS.
- Reggie Helm: lawyer for TS and The Covenant; Dom/husband of Colleen.
- Alyssa Wagner: teenager saved by Jake from an abusive father; lives with Rick and Eileen.
- Carl Talbot: college professor; Dom and Whip Master at The Covenant.

The Omega Team and Their Significant Others

- Cain "Shades" Foster: retired Secret Service agent.

- Tristan "Duracell" McCabe: retired Army Special Forces.
- Logan "Cowboy" Reese: retired Marine Special Forces; former prisoner of war; boyfriend/Dom of Dakota.
- Valentino "Romeo" Mancini: retired Army Special Forces; former FBI Hostage Rescue Team (HRT) member.
- Darius "Batman" Knight: retired Navy SEAL.
- Kip "Skipper" Morrison: retired Army; former LAPD SWAT sniper.
- Lindsey "Costello" Abbott: retired Marine; sniper.
- Dakota Swift: Tampa PD undercover police officer; submissive/girlfriend of Logan.

Trident Support Staff

- Colleen McKinley Helm: office manager of TS; wife/submissive of Reggie.
- Tempest "Babs" Van Buren: retired Air Force helicopter pilot; TS mechanic.
- Russell Adams: retired Navy; assistant TS mechanic.
- Nathan Cook: former computer specialist with the National Security Agency (NSA).

Members of Law Enforcement

- Larry Keon: Assistant Director of the FBI.

- Frank Stonewall: Special Agent in Charge of the Tampa FBI.
- Calvin Watts: Leader of the FBI HRT in Tampa.
- Colt Parrish: Major Case Specialist, Behavioral Analysis Unit.

The K9s of Trident

- Beau: An orphaned Lab/Pit mix, rescued by Ian. Now a trained K9 who has more than earned his spot on the Alpha Team. Has been assigned to now watch over Kristen, Angie, JD, and any other children that join the family.
- Spanky: A rescued Bullmastiff, with a heart of gold, owned by Parker and Shelby.
- Jagger: A rescued Rottweiler trained as an assistance/service animal for Russell.
- FUBAR: A Belgian Malinois who failed aggressive guard dog training. Adopted by Babs.
- BDSM: Bravo, Delta, Sierra, and Mike, two Belgian Malinoises and two German shepherds, the new guard dogs at the Trident compound that Ian named using the military communication's alphabet.

PART TWO
CHARACTER PROFILES

Some of the categories are based on suggestions from the members of The Sexy Six-Pack's Sirens Facebook group. Ages and other statistics are based on books released before November 2018. Only couples from the original TS series and the Doms of The Covenant series, who have had their happy ever after, are included in this section. Characters from the Omega Team, Deimos series, and others will be listed in future volumes of the field manual. List of characters is in book-release order.

Devon Sawyer:

Age: 39

Place of Birth: Charlotte, NC

Birth Month: January

Nickname: Devil Dog

Siblings: Ian, Nick, and John (deceased)
Retired rank from Navy: Ensign
SEAL Team Expert/Position: lead climber, lead breacher
Height: 6'2"
Hair color: black
Eye color: blue
Tattoo: brother John's initials, date of birth and date of death over heart
Vehicle: 1966 Ford Mustang Convertible; Ford Expedition
Favorite pizza: sausage, mushroom, and onions
Favorite ice cream: rocky road
Favorite baked goods from Fancy's bakery: fruit tarts
Least favorite food: liver
Favorite color: blue
Favorite BDSM toy/piece of equipment: flogger
Favorite Music Genre: country
Favorite Movie: *Die Hard*
Favorite Guilty-Pleasure Reality TV Show: *Hell's Kitchen*
Random Fact: Had a childhood crush on Xena the Princess Warrior and even wrote her a fan letter at eight years old.

Kristen Sawyer:
Age: 29
Place of Birth: New Hope, PA
Maiden Name: Anders
Siblings: two step-brothers who live in Pennsylvania
Birth Month: July
Nickname: Ninja-girl
Height: 5'6"
Hair Color: Brown

Eye Color: Hazel

Career: indie/traditional-hybrid author; NYT and USA Today Bestselling Author

Vehicle: Chrysler Town & Country

Favorite pizza: extra cheese

Favorite ice cream: mint chocolate chip

Favorite baked goods from Fancy's bakery: crumb cake

Least favorite food: Brussel sprouts

Favorite color: purple

Favorite BDSM toy/piece of equipment: bullet vibrator or vibrating panties

Favorite Music Genre: easy listening

Favorite Movie: *Steel Magnolias*

Favorite Guilty-Pleasure Reality TV Show: *Dancing with the Stars*

Random Fact: Appeared on the *Ellen DeGeneres Show*.

Ian Sawyer:

Age: 41

Place of Birth: Charlotte, NC

Birth Month: June

Nickname: Boss-man

Siblings: Devon, Nick, and John (deceased)

Retired rank from Navy: Lieutenant

SEAL Team Expert/Position: Advanced Special Operations and interrogator

Height: 6'2"

Hair color: black

Eye color: blue

Scar: bullet wound, left side of chest, just above heart

Vehicle: Audi RS5 Coupe; Ford Expedition
Favorite pizza: onions and bacon
Favorite ice cream: butter pecan
Favorite baked goods from Fancy's bakery: pecan rolls
Least favorite food: anchovies
Favorite color: green
Favorite BDSM toy/piece of equipment: nipple clamps
Favorite Music Genre: classic rock and roll
Favorite Movie: *The Godfather*
Favorite Guilty-Pleasure Reality TV Show: *Deadliest Catch*
Random Fact: Dated/Topped Supermodel Savanah McCall
while still in the Navy.

Angelina Sawyer:
Age: 36
Place of Birth: Lake George, NY
Birth Month: September
Maiden Name: Beckett
Nicknames: Angie/Angel
Height: 5'8"
Hair color: blonde
Eye color: green
Siblings: brother, Sam—deceased
Vehicle: Chrysler Pacifica
Favorite pizza: chicken parmesan
Favorite ice cream: chocolate chip cookie dough
Favorite baked goods from Fancy's bakery: rainbow cookies
Least favorite food: cauliflower
Favorite color: red
Favorite BDSM toy/piece of equipment: spreader bar

Favorite Music Genre: pop music
Favorite Movie: *Titanic*
Favorite Guilty-Pleasure Reality TV Show: *The Voice*
Random Fact: Has sold several paintings through a local art gallery. Sketches veterans recovering from devastating injuries in combat.

Benjamin Michaelson:
Age: 33
Place of Birth: Norfolk, VA
Birth Month: May
Nicknames: Boomer or Baby Boomer
Sibling: foster sister, Alyssa Wagner
Retired rank from Navy: Petty Officer 1st Class
SEAL Team Expert/Position: Explosive Ordnance Disposal
Height: 6'1"
Hair color: dark brown
Eye color: amber
Scars: left knee and leg from RPG attack
Vehicle: Dodge Charger
Favorite pizza: everything, including anchovies
Favorite ice cream: cherry vanilla
Favorite baked goods from Fancy's bakery: cannoli
Least favorite food: Doesn't have one—will eat practically anything
Favorite color: navy blue
Favorite BDSM toy/piece of equipment: spanking bench
Favorite Music Genre: rock and roll or heavy metal
Favorite Movie: *Silence of the Lambs*
Favorite Guilty-Pleasure Reality TV Show: *Pit Bulls & Parolees*

Random Fact: Still has all his Legos from when he was a boy
—saving them for his own kids.

Katerina Michaelson:

Age: 32

Place of Birth: Norfolk, VA

Birth Month: December

Maiden Name: Maier

Nicknames: Kat/Kitten/Kitty Kat

Sibling: brother, Alex—deceased

Height: 5'5"

Hair color: light brown

Eye color: brown

Vehicle: Nissan Pathfinder

Favorite pizza: ricotta, mozzarella, and spinach

Favorite ice cream: key lime pie

Favorite baked goods from Fancy's bakery: cheesecake

Least favorite food: clams and oysters

Favorite color: teal

Favorite BDSM toy/piece of equipment: flogger

Favorite Music Genre: country or pop music

Favorite Movie: *Miracle on 34th Street* (1947)

Favorite Guilty-Pleasure Reality TV Show: *America's Got
Talent*

Random Fact: Retrieved father's ashes from the cemetery
where he was interred in Portland, OR, and buried them next
to her mother and brother in Norfolk, VA.

Parker Christiansen:

Age: 33

Place of Birth: Boston, MA

Birth Month: March

Height: 5'11"

Hair color: dirty blond

Eye color: Brown

Sibling: Dave—estranged

Vehicle: Ford F-150

Pet: Spanky (bullmastiff)

Favorite pizza: buffalo chicken

Favorite ice cream: rum raisin

Favorite baked goods from Fancy's bakery: double fudge brownies

Least favorite food: anything with curry

Favorite color: pink (when Shelby wears it)

Favorite BDSM toy/piece of equipment: nipple and clit clamps

Favorite Music Genre: classic rock and roll

Favorite Movie: *The Good, the Bad, and the Ugly*

Favorite Guilty-Pleasure Reality TV Show: *Survivor*

Random Fact: Loves taking his sons to the zoo, aquarium, and other fun places that he didn't get to go to as a kid because his parents couldn't be bothered with spending time with their children.

Shelby Christiansen:

Age: 32

Place of Birth: Dearborn, MI

Birth Month: April

Maiden Name: Whitman

Sibling: Shannon—currently living in Nevada

Height: 5'4"
Hair color: blonde
Eye color: hazel
Vehicle: Kia Sedona
Favorite pizza: pepperoni
Favorite ice cream: Dulce de Leche
Favorite baked goods from Fancy's bakery: linzer tarts
Least favorite food: sweet potatoes
Favorite color: any color in the rainbow
Favorite BDSM toy/piece of equipment: Ben-Wa balls
Favorite Music Genre: pop music, 90s
Favorite Movie: *Casablanca*
Favorite Guilty-Pleasure Reality TV Show: *Dancing with the Stars*
Random Fact: Joined the PTA—something she never thought she'd be able to do.

Jake Donovan:
Age: 37
Place of Birth: Tampa, FL
Birth Month: June
Height: 6'5"
Hair color: medium brown
Eye color: green
Scars: small scar on the outside of left eye, multiple crescent-shaped scars on back
Sibling: Michael
Nickname: Reverend
Retired rank from Navy: Master Chief
SEAL Team Expert/Position: Sniper

Vehicle: Chevy Suburban

Favorite pizza: plain cheese

Favorite ice cream: pistachio

Favorite baked goods from Fancy's bakery: cannolis

Least favorite food: deviled eggs

Favorite color: blue

Favorite BDSM toy/piece of equipment: bullwhip

Favorite Music Genre: classic rock and roll, jazz, Celtic

Favorite Movie: *Young Frankenstein*

Favorite Guilty-Pleasure Reality TV Show: Doesn't have one —prefers shows on the History and Travel Channels.

Random Fact: Enjoys reading non-fiction history and biographies.

Nick Donovan:

Age: 28

Place of Birth: Charlotte, NC

Birth Month: January

Height: 6'1"

Hair color: Black

Eye color: Blue

Scars: Bullet wound and surgery scar on left chest under clavicle, appendectomy

Birth surname: Sawyer

Nickname: Junior

Retired rank from Navy: Petty Officer 2nd Class

SEAL Team Expert/Position: Point-man/Navigator

Vehicle: Ford F-150

Favorite pizza: buffalo chicken

Favorite ice cream: Moose Tracks

Favorite baked goods from Fancy's bakery: black and white cookies
Least favorite food: olives
Favorite color: green
Favorite BDSM toy: crop
Least Favorite BDSM toy: ginger plug and cock cage
Favorite Music Genre: pop and rap, but not gangsta rap
Favorite Movie: *The Matrix*
Favorite Guilty-Pleasure Reality TV Show: *Shark Tank*
Random Fact: Started training for next year's Iron Man Competition

Marco DeAngelis:
Age: 38
Place of Birth: Staten Island, NY
Birth Month: April
Height: 6'2"
Hair color: black
Sibling: Nina—deceased
Tattoos: Angel tattoo with butterfly wings and Nina's and Mara's names on upper left arm. Fancy triskelion with Harper's name on upper right arm.
Nickname: Polo
Retired rank from Navy: Chief
SEAL Team Expert/Position: Communications, Air Operations Master, backup helicopter pilot
Vehicle: Chevy Silverado
Favorite Sports Teams: NY Giants, NY Mets, NY Rangers
Favorite pizza: NY style extra cheese
Favorite ice cream: chocolate marshmallow

Favorite baked goods from Fancy's bakery: cannoli

Least favorite food: split pea soup

Favorite color: ocean blue

Favorite BDSM play: wax play

Favorite Music Genre: rock and roll

Favorite Movie: *Mad Max*

Favorite Guilty-Pleasure Reality TV Show: *Expedition Unknown*

Random Fact: His daughter's giggle is his favorite sound in the whole world (next to Harper screaming his name when she orgasms).

Harper DeAngelis:

Age: 34

Place of Birth: Clearwater, FL

Birth Month: April

Siblings: none

Height: 5'9"

Hair color: light blonde

Eye color: hazel

Vehicle: Subaru Forester

Favorite pizza: bacon and onions

Favorite ice cream: mint chocolate chip

Favorite baked goods from Fancy's bakery: linter tarts

Least favorite food: celery

Favorite color: pink

Favorite BDSM toy/piece of equipment: nipple clamps

Favorite Music Genre: anything but heavy rap and punk rock

Favorite Movie: *Sense & Sensibility*

Favorite Guilty-Pleasure Reality TV Show: *The Voice*

Random Fact: Watching the TV show *Law & Order* as a teen influenced decision to become a lawyer

Curt Bannerman:
Age: 42
Place of Birth: Daytona, FL
Birth Month: June
Sibling: brother, Chris
Height: 6'4"
Hair color: blond
Eye color: blue
Scars: left bicep, right thigh, right shoulder
Nickname: Elmer
Retired rank from Navy: Chief
Team Expert in: Weapons
Vehicle: Harley Davidson Softail Deluxe, Ford F-150
Favorite pizza: meat lovers
Favorite ice cream: cherry vanilla
Least favorite food: MREs
Favorite color: red
Favorite Music Genre: country
Favorite Movie: *Blazing Saddles*
Favorite Guilty-Pleasure Reality TV Show: *Deadliest Catch*
Random Fact: Learned to ride a motorcycle before learning to drive a car.

Dana Pritchard-Bannerman:
Age: 41
Place of Birth: Wright-Patterson Air Force Base, Greene County, OH

Birth Month: November

Maiden Name: Goodman

Siblings: none

Height: 5'8"

Hair color: brown

Eye color: brown

Vehicle: Ford Escape

Favorite pizza: extra cheese

Favorite ice cream: Dulce de Leche

Least favorite food: liver

Favorite color: green

Favorite Music Genre: pop music, 90s, country

Favorite Movie: *It's a Wonderful Life*

Favorite Guilty-Pleasure Reality TV Show: *The Voice*

Random Fact: Loves watching Christmas cartoons every year —favorite is *A Charlie Brown Christmas*.

Brody Evans:

Age: 38

Place of Birth: Dallas, TX

Birth Month: May

Height: 6'2"

Hair color: blond

Eye color: brown

Scars/distinguishing marks: small toe on right was amputated

Nickname: Egghead, Frodo

Retired rank from Navy: Senior Chief

SEAL Team Expert/Position: Technical Surveillance, Computer Specialist

Vehicle: Ford F-150

Favorite Sports Team(s): Dallas Cowboys, Texas Rangers

Favorite pizza: pepperoni

Favorite ice cream: rocky road

Favorite baked goods from Fancy's bakery: Anything—including the baker

Least favorite food: kale

Favorite color: black

Favorite BDSM toy/piece of equipment: spanking bench

Favorite Music Genre: country and classic rock

Favorite Movie: *Lord of the Rings Trilogy*

Favorite Guilty-Pleasure Reality TV Show: *Pawn Stars*

Random Fact: Read the Lord of the Rings Trilogy at ten years old.

Francine Evans:

Age: 32

Place of Birth: Westlake, OH

Birth Month: January

Maiden Name: Bayles

Surname from First Marriage: McGuire

Nickname: Fancy

Height: 5'4"

Hair color: auburn

Eye color: green

Vehicle: Dodge Grand Caravan

Favorite Sports Team: Cleveland Indians

Favorite pizza: salad pizza

Favorite ice cream: strawberry

Least favorite food: Swiss cheese

Favorite color: blue

Favorite BDSM toy/piece of equipment: violet wand

Favorite Music Genre: pop music and country

Favorite Movie: *Steel Magnolias*

Favorite Guilty-Pleasure Reality TV Show: *Dancing with the Stars*

Random Fact: Addicted to *Candy Crush* on phone.

T. Carter:

Age: 40

Place of Birth: Classified location in California

Birth Month: September

Sibling: foster sister, Vicki

Height: 6'4"

Hair color: dark blond

Eye color: blue

Scars: several small scars on arms, torso, legs—nothing too distinguishable

Alias: Carter Burke

Vehicles: Dodge Challenger—Tampa, Ram 1500—Montana, and dozens of other vehicles stored around the world.

Favorite pizza: everything but anchovies and the kitchen sink

Favorite ice cream: fudge ripple

Favorite baked goods from Fancy's bakery: blueberry or cinnamon apple muffins

Least favorite food: mayonnaise

Favorite color: blue

Favorite BDSM toy/piece of equipment: Their sex swing gets a lot of use, and he likes a ball gag for when Jordyn needs to be punished.

Favorite Music Genre: classic rock and roll
Favorite Movie: *Scarface*
Favorite Guilty-Pleasure Reality TV Show: Seriously?
Random Fact: Has over fifty residences in various countries around the world.

Jordyn Alvarez:
Age: 34
Place of Birth: Buenos Aires, Argentina
Birth Month: April
Siblings: none
Height: 5'4"
Hair color: black
Eye color: brown
Vehicle: Too many to count around the world but her favorites are a Bugatti Veyron 16.4 and a '67 Camaro.
Favorite pizza: chicken Alfredo
Favorite ice cream: Dulce de Leche
Favorite baked goods from Fancy's bakery: Boston creme pie
Least favorite food: fast food hamburgers
Favorite color: black
Least Favorite BDSM toy: ball gag
Favorite BDSM piece of equipment: sex swing
Favorite Music Genre: Latina, pop
Favorite Movie: *Casablanca*
Favorite Guilty-Pleasure Reality TV Show: *America's Got Talent*
Random Fact: Hates to cook.

Grayson Mann:

Age: 36
Place of Birth: St. Petersburg, FL
Birth Month: October
Sibling: Remington
Height: 6'3"
Hair color: dark brown
Eye color: hazel
Scars: one-inch scar along hairline
Vehicle: BMW i8
Favorite pizza: margherita
Favorite ice cream: Phish Food
Favorite baked goods from Fancy's bakery: oatmeal raisin cookies
Least favorite food: avocados
Favorite color: red and black
Favorite BDSM toy/piece of equipment: anal toys
Favorite Music Genre: classic rock and roll
Favorite Movie: *Monty Python and the Holy Grail*
Favorite Guilty-Pleasure Reality TV Show: *Duck Dynasty*
Random Fact: He constantly reminds Remi that he's the oldest by a minute.

Abigail Turner:
Age: 30
Place of Birth: St. Petersburg, FL
Birth Month: March
Nickname: Abbie
Height: 5'6"
Hair color: golden brown
Eye color: brown

Vehicle: Audi Q5
Favorite pizza: vegetable
Favorite ice cream: coffee
Favorite baked goods from Fancy's bakery: scones—any flavor
Least favorite food: pumpkin
Favorite color: purple
Favorite BDSM toy/piece of equipment: Loves being blind-folded and restrained
Favorite Music Genre: country and pop
Favorite Movie: *Breakfast at Tiffany's*
Favorite Guilty-Pleasure Reality TV Show: *Long Island Medium*
Random Fact: Has read all the Harry Potter books

Remington Mann:
Age: 36
Place of Birth: St. Petersburg, FL
Birth Month: October
Sibling: Grayson
Height: 6'2"
Hair color: dark brown
Eye color: brown
Scars: appendectomy
Vehicle: Porsche Cayenne Turbo S
Favorite pizza: shrimp and clam scampi
Favorite ice cream: cookies and cream
Favorite baked goods from Fancy's bakery: seven-layer cake
Least favorite food: broccoli
Favorite color: blue

Favorite BDSM toy/piece of equipment: nipple clamps, wax play

Favorite Music Genre: classic rock and roll

Favorite Movie: all the *Fast & Furious* movies

Favorite Guilty-Pleasure Reality TV Show: *American Ninja Warrior*

Random Fact: Was the one to convince Gray they should take a shot at the music business.

Mitch Sawyer:

Age: 35

Place of Birth: Palm Harbor, FL

Birth Month: February

Sibling: brother—Dan, Jr—DJ

Height: 6'0"

Hair color: Black

Eye color: Blue

Vehicle: BMW X5

Favorite pizza: meat lovers

Favorite ice cream: chocolate chip cookie dough

Favorite baked goods from Fancy's bakery: cannolis

Least favorite food: cauliflower

Favorite color: ocean blue

Favorite BDSM toy/piece of equipment: butt plug and St. Andrew's cross

Favorite Music Genre: pop, country, rock, rap

Favorite Movie: *Goodfellas*

Favorite Guilty-Pleasure Reality TV Show: *American Ninja Warriors*

Random Fact: Likes to SCUBA dive historic wrecks in Gulf and Keys.

Tyler Ellis:
Age: 34
Place of Birth: Tampa, FL
Birth Month: August
Sibling: brother, Tom; sister, Stephanie
Height: 5'11"
Hair color: brown
Eye color: hazel
Scars: left shin
Tattoo: BDSM symbol on left shoulder blade, serpent wrapped around sword on left side of chest, "In Truth Is Strength" on right side of torso, tribal design on right side of chest
Vehicle: BMW 6 Series Gran Turismo
Favorite pizza: meat lover's
Favorite ice cream: maple walnut
Favorite baked goods from Fancy's bakery: cinnamon rolls
Least favorite food: egg salad
Favorite color: red
Favorite BDSM toy/piece of equipment: clamps, restraints, cock ring
Favorite Music Genre: rap, pop
Favorite Movie: *Iron Man*
Favorite Guilty-Pleasure Reality TV Show: *Diners, Drive-ins, Dives*
Random Fact: Taking sailing lessons. Wants to buy a sailboat.

Tori Freyja:

Age: 31

Place of Birth: Grand Rapids, MI

Birth Month: April

Siblings: none

Height: 5'6"

Hair color: dark blonde

Eye color: brown

Scars: Right forearm from bite received while breaking up a dog fight

Vehicle: Nissan Quest

Favorite pizza: bacon, chicken, ranch

Favorite ice cream: Moose Tracks

Favorite baked goods from Fancy's bakery: apple pie

Least favorite food: oysters

Favorite color: orange

Favorite BDSM toy/piece of equipment: Vibrator, flogger, sensation play

Favorite Music Genre: rock and roll, rap

Favorite Movie: Anything with Matt Damon in it

Favorite Guilty-Pleasure Reality TV Show: *The Pioneer Woman*

Random Fact: Queen of Trivial Pursuit

Jase Atwood:

Age: 36

Place of Birth: Classified

Birth Month: Classified

Sibling: Classified

Birth Name: Classified

Height: 6'1"

Hair color: light brown

Eye color: dark brown

Scars: bullet wound under left arm,

Vehicle: Jeep Wrangler, Suzuki V-Strom DL650

Favorite pizza: barbecue chicken

Favorite ice cream: raspberry ripple

Least favorite food: grits

Favorite color: teal blue

Favorite BDSM play: ice play

Favorite Music Genre: rock and roll, reggae

Favorite Movie: *The Shawshank Redemption*

Favorite Guilty-Pleasure Reality TV Show: Doesn't watch much TV on Caicos but used to watch *Pawn Stars* in the States.

Random Fact: Talking to Ian, Devon, Carter, and Mistress Cara about opening a BDSM club on Caicos—one, to have a safe place for people to play, and two, to have a place for operatives from around the world to exchange intel.

Brie Hanson:

Age: 33

Place of Birth: Fort Myers, FL

Birth Month: March

Sibling: sister, Nadine

Height: 5'11"

Hair color: blonde

Eye color: green

Vehicle: Jeep Wrangler

Favorite snack: nachos

Favorite ice cream: vanilla and chocolate swirl

Least favorite food: pork and beans

Favorite color: purple

Favorite BDSM play: sensation play

Favorite Music Genre: 80s and 90s pop and rock

Favorite Movie: *The Wizard of Oz*

Favorite Guilty-Pleasure Reality TV Show: She works most nights, so doesn't really watch reality TV, but does watch a few Netflix shows.

Random Fact: Hates social media—only goes on Facebook to check in with Angie and the other women of Trident.

Charlotte Roth:

Age: 35

Place of Birth: Englewood, NJ

Birth Month: March

Siblings: sister, Caroline; brother, David

Height: 5'3"

Hair color: black

Eye color: brown

Vehicle: Chevy Tahoe

Pet: Confucius (cat)

Favorite pizza: thin-crust sausage and peppers

Favorite ice cream: believe it or not—vanilla

Favorite baked goods from Fancy's bakery: double fudge brownies

Least favorite food: Brussel sprouts

Favorite color: red

Favorite BDSM toy/piece of equipment: bullwhip

Favorite Music Genre: 80s, 90s, pop

Favorite Movie: *Good Will Hunting*
Favorite Guilty-Pleasure Reality TV Show: *Say Yes to the Dress*
Random Fact: Loves to cook and experiment with recipes.

Michael Donovan:
Age: 39
Place of Birth: Tampa, FL
Birth Month: September
Sibling: brother, Jake
Height: 6'0"
Hair color: light brown
Eye color: hazel
Vehicle: GMC Terrain
Favorite pizza: buffalo chicken
Favorite ice cream: butter pecan
Favorite baked goods from Fancy's bakery: blondies
Least favorite food: raw sushi
Favorite color: green
Favorite BDSM toy/piece of equipment: flogger
Favorite Music Genre: rock, Celtic, pop
Favorite Movie: *Pulp Fiction*
Favorite Guilty-Pleasure Reality TV Show: *Survivor*
Random Fact: Addicted to *Smash Hit* app on phone

PART THREE
Q&A

Members of the Sexy Six-Pack's Sirens Facebook group had an opportunity to question the Trident Security teams, members of The Covenant, and their families and friends. The following is the resulting online Q&A session. Some answers may contain spoilers for books written before November 1, 2018.

Please say hello to the TS gang, their family, and their friends.

Rhonda B.: For any of the guys or gals . . . when did you realize you were a Dominant or a submissive?

Shelby: Back in college, I went to a munch with some friends, thinking it would be a fun girl's night out. Honestly, I'd thought the lifestyle was something to laugh at before I went there. We thought we'd be seeing a bunch of half-naked people participating in role play like puppy play or something. But part of the event included a Dom and a sub giving a presentation. While they just talked and explained things, without any play, I found myself drawn more and more to their words. I sought them out after the presentation to ask them a bunch of questions I suddenly had. Of course, a lot of other people wanted to talk to them too, so I had to wait in a line, but they took the time to talk to each of us. When I finally introduced myself to the Dom, I felt a sense of peace come over me. He was one of those ideal Doms you read about in romance novels—no joke. He was caring about all subs, not just his own. He stressed safe, sane, and consensual, and explained the difference between a Dom you wanted to find vs. a wannabe-Dom who didn't get it and was in the lifestyle for all the wrong reasons. Before the night was over, I was hooked. I just knew I had to give the lifestyle a try.

Jessica Z.: This is for any of the guys—who introduced you to the lifestyle?

Master Cain: I found the lifestyle completely by accident while on the job. As a Secret Service agent, I had to follow those I was protecting into some very strange places. At one point in my career, I was assigned to a high-ranking official's daughter. She was, and still is, a member of Club X in the Georgetown area of Washington D.C. and went there often.

Hence, I went there often as well. It didn't take me long to get into the lifestyle after that, and, no, I never played while on a detail.

Leia M.: This is for anyone—how can someone tell their partner they want to learn how to be a submissive?

Fancy: I'll take this question. If you've read about my background, then you know I'd dabbled in the lifestyle before I'd ever met Brody. But that was not the case with my first-husband, Patrick. I was the one to approach him about it after one of my girlfriends had told me about how she and her husband had been in the lifestyle for a year or two. It was scary at first—I wasn't sure what he knew about BDSM or how he felt about it. I did a lot of research and enlisted our friends' help. The husband started mentioning the lifestyle among the four of us and in one-on-one conversations with Patrick, so it wouldn't be a foreign subject when I approached him about it. Then, one night, lying in bed, I brought it up, using our friends' descriptions of the lifestyle as an ice breaker. I was happy to find he wasn't as shocked as he could have been without being eased into it. Unfortunately, we'd only just started exploring the lifestyle before Patrick was killed. When Brody told me he was a Dom, I don't know, it almost felt like Patrick had sent someone for me to love again—someone who was perfect for me.

Terra O.: Devon, do you think you and Carter connect more together than any of the others in Trident Security, since you have done scenes together with Kristen and some other subs?

Devon: I'm not the only Alpha Team member who's had a ménage with Carter. Boomer has too, and I think one or two of the other guys. Ian hasn't.

Speaking for myself, though, I'd developed a close relationship with Carter over the years before we'd ever shared a woman. In our business, trust must be earned—lives depend upon it. I think we were able to take the trust that's between us on missions and roll it over into something personal. Actually, those types of trust are both personal but in different ways. Carter has earned my respect as a teammate, a Dom, and a friend over the years. If I had even a sliver of doubt that he would harm Kristen in any way, shape, or form, I would never have invited him to share my beautiful sub.

Kelle B: For Ian—what's your fondest childhood memory and why?

Ian: My brothers and I had a great childhood. Dad didn't start out rich—he earned it through blood, sweat, and tears. I think we turned out the way we have because of his work ethics. I admire my dad more than any other man on this earth. My fondest memories are when he took a day off from work now and then—he'd started as a real estate agent—and took my brothers and me out of school.

He'd take us fishing, but it was never about the fish. It was about bonding with his sons. We had some of the best conversations while fishing—still do. When my kids are old enough, fishing is going to be something I'll do with them as often as I can.

Janet H.: Chuck and Marie Sawyer, do you have a Dom/sub relationship?

Marie: No, we do not. We've always been on equal terms both in and out of the bedroom. But we've also learned each other has particular strengths, at times, and we can let them take the reins for a bit. When our sons first told us they were opening a club, you can imagine our surprise. But, like any good doctor, I did the research and shared it with Chuck. We began to understand why people got into the lifestyle and what they got out of it. We also understand and learned there are clubs like this all over the world, and many aren't safe for the members. Ian, Devon, and Mitch stressed they wanted a safe haven for those who wanted to explore the lifestyle they'd come to be a part of. I'm proud of them, just don't ask me to go into the club, lol. I prefer to keep some images of my sons and nephew out of my head.

Kelle B.: For Carter—my question is the same as the one I gave Ian. What is your fondest childhood memory and why?

Carter: As you probably know, I didn't have a

great childhood. But I'd have to say, my fondest memory is from a few days after I met my foster sister Vicki. I was a broody kid, as you can imagine. Being shuffled from foster home to foster home doesn't give you many reasons *not* to be broody. Anyway, I was in the backyard hitting pebbles with a bat, since there wasn't a ball, when Vicki came outside. She had a package of Twinkies with her—I don't even remember where she got the money for them. She sat down, opened them, and offered me one. I was surprised and asked her why—I was so used to other kids being stingy with the things they had because most of us had so little. She said, "Because Twinkies make me smile, and you need a reason to smile." I knew she would be special to me from that moment on.

Mary G.: Carter, what is your favorite food?

Carter: That goes with the last question—Twinkies.

Boomer: Yeah, "I'm just here for the Twinkies" doesn't work for me. Glad you went with the standard line.

Mary G.: Tiny, what do you enjoy most about working at The Covenant?

Tiny: While I'm not in the lifestyle, as you know, I do feel the need to protect women. I like knowing that I'll be there if they need me. And having them wear skimpy outfits doesn't hurt—just kidding.

Anyway, it'd started out as just a job, but the friendships I've developed with the members has made it so much more than that—it's a family.

Pauline H.: Jordyn, what is the fondest childhood memory you have?

Jordyn: As you can imagine, there are many parts of my childhood that were filled with things I'd rather not remember. But I can still recall my mother singing me to sleep many nights. She was a beauty queen and had a lyrical voice. After she was gone and I went to the orphanage, I was lucky enough to have Sister Patrice. She also loved to sing and would often do so when I couldn't sleep at night. Sharing that time with both of them are my fondest memories.

Tawnya W.: For Ian—cloth diapers or disposable?

Ian: I hate doing laundry! Disposable. (Please don't tell the environmentalists!)

Lee G.: Carter, how do you appear and disappear so easily and be exactly where you need to be when someone needs you? Are you psychic?

Carter: Sorry to sound cliché, but if I tell you, I'd have to kill you—just kidding. Actually, I'm not psychic in the way some yahoos say they are, but I do get vibes when something's not kosher, and it's a good thing I've learned to listen to them.

Tawnya W.: Jake, when are you and Nick gonna become parents?

Jake: We've talked about it. I'm not sure if and when it'll happen because it's going to cause some huge changes in our lives and jobs. We'll want to be on separate teams if we do become parents, in case a mission goes FUBAR. It's a sad reality that both of us could be killed on the same mission, so we would want to avoid that at all costs. The good thing is we have such a supportive extended family who have already expressed their desire to help us in any way if we do start a family of our own. By the way, that can't happen soon enough for my mom. She's the queen of dropping hints about wanting to become a grandmother. I hope Charlotte and Mike get married and start a family soon to take some of the heat off Nick and me.

Charlotte: Nothing like throwing us under the bus, Jake. Thanks.

Jake: No problem. I'm sure you'll return the *favor* someday soon.

Allena H.: Carter and Jordyn, when will you guys retire your current roles and slow down?

Carter: We have no plans to slow down just yet. We both get a little stir crazy if we've been sitting too long without a mission.

Autumn W.: My question is also for Carter and

Jordyn. Do you see yourselves getting married and having children anytime soon?

Jordyn: A baby is something we've talked about, but we'd need to make some drastic changes in our careers that neither one of us are willing to make right now. I've told him when the time comes to have kids, I want both our asses on US soil as much as possible. We're not quite sure what we're going to do to make that happen though.

Carter: As for getting married, I'm sure there'll be an announcement someday.

Tawnya W.: Carter, wanna babysit in the meantime? You and Jordyn would be great!

Carter: Sure! Oddly, since we both had crappy childhoods, we both love kids. I didn't get to see my nephew too often while he was growing up, so I cherish the times I can spend with him.

Rhonda B.: Brody, what is your favorite dessert that Fancy bakes?

Brody: Everything! But if I had to pick just one, it would be her strawberry shortcake. Thank God I married a woman who can satisfy my sweet tooth and then help me work off the extra calories!

Terry K.: Also for Brody—what are you looking forward to the most about being a dad?

Brody: The most? Holding my kid for the first time. I love my nieces and nephews, but watching my child grow inside my Fancy-girl is the most amazing experience in the world!

Sam T.: For Carter—which boyhood nemesis are you most likely to tie to a chair and feed Naga chilis?

Carter: Naga chilis, huh? I like that idea. As for who I'd what to do it to, well, that's easy. I was about nine years old and a fourteen-year-old jackass, who was the biological child of the foster parents I was living with at the time, forced me to eat a full jar of mayonnaise—I puked for hours after that. Hence the reason I can't stand the stuff today. There have been moments I've thought of tracking him down, but my conscience won't let me, since I'll want to use a few tricks on him I've learned over the years. I guarantee it wouldn't be pretty.

Rhonda B: Abby, will you continue to work for Gray and Remi if you three have children?

Abby: Yes! I've already talked them into adding a childcare center to the company. We'll be renovating an area one floor below the executive offices of BDR. Remi and Gray only agreed to it if I swore I'd take six-weeks maternity leave after having any children.

Dawn S.: For Kristen, I have two questions. One—for not being in the BDSM lifestyle at the beginning, how did you let go of any sexual insecurities or body image insecurities, if you had any? And, two—what goes through your mind when you're wearing close to nothing and you and Devon go to The Covenant?

Kristen: Oh, I definitely had body image and sexual insecurities, and if it hadn't been for Devon knowing that, without me coming right out and telling him at first, I don't think I would've ever gotten past them. I'm not one-hundred percent comfortable in my skin yet—Devon knows that—and I'm not sure if I ever will be. My ex's voice still pops into my head, at times, making me doubt things. But my husband understands all that, and he does his best to make me see that I'm beautiful to him in every way. He loves my body, stretch marks and all after having JD, and that makes me appreciate my curves and perceived flaws even more. As for the sexual insecurities, yeah, he tosses those out the window with every orgasm he gives me. I love sex more than ever!

For the second question, that falls back on my answer above. I'll never be one hundred percent comfortable, but I have gotten much better. Devon's attention on me at the club gives me something else to think about. Surprisingly, my worries about what people are thinking when they see my body aren't about the men, but about what other women are thinking and saying. I guess that goes back to my teenage years, when every girl wanted to be in with the cool kids, instead of being someone they were whispering about when it came to clothes, hair, makeup, weight, height, etc. But most of the women in the club have the same thoughts at times, and some of us do talk about it and try to reassure each other we're all beautiful in our own ways.

Terry K.: This is for Devon—being a Dom and wanting to keep Kristen from being hurt, how did you handle the birth of JD?

Kristen: He didn't handle it well at all! LOL!

Devon: Quiet, you little brat—the question was directed to me. She's right, though. It just about killed me seeing her in pain. I almost got kicked out of the delivery room for yelling at them to do something, anything to reduce the amount of pain she was in. But seeing her smile, as the nurse handed her JD for the first time, made it all worth it.

Helena H.: To Ian—if you could tell people not in the BDSM community one thing they should know about it, what would it be?

Ian: Without a doubt, the one thing anyone trying the lifestyle must understand is that everything must be safe, sane, and consensual. If it's not, RUN! What's portrayed in a lot of books and movies lately is not always accurate. There are a lot of people using the excuse of the lifestyle to abuse others.

Linda M.: Jordyn, I would like to ask about Carter.

Jordyn: What would you like to know about Master Asshole? I'm mad at him at the moment because, while I'm typing this, I have a ball gag in my mouth and a butt plug up my ass, and he's laughing at me.

Linda: Never mind.

Tawnya W.: Shelby, I have a two-part question for you. How does it feel to now have your boys? And do you and Parker think you'll be adding a girl to your family?

Shelby: I absolutely love my boys! I can't remember life without them, although they do keep me on my toes! Spanky has slept in their bedroom every night since we brought them home. They're doing well in school. The fact that Sister Patrice made sure the kids at the orphanage learned both Spanish and English has helped tremendously. But the boys have figured out that we don't understand a lot of Spanish (which we're trying to fix with a Spanish teaching program), so we have to remind them it's not polite. We've also been using a translation app on our phones when they try to pull one over on us. By the way, Spanky now knows "sit," "stay," "lie down," "fetch," and "cookie" in Spanish.

While we have no plans at the moment to adopt again, I do think at some point we'll try to add a little girl to our family.

Helena H.: Boomer, when the love of your life was taken away, you must have had dreams of what life would've been like with her. Now that she's returned to you, is it what you envisioned?

Boomer: Any dream I'd had of her when I thought she was gone forever doesn't come close to what it's like having Kitten back in my life. I know I'm a bit of a unicorn, having the love of my life, who I thought was dead, come back and give me a second chance, and I'll never forget how blessed I am to have her in my arms again.

Ame S.: Devon, if John hadn't died and you'd continued with your college education, do you think you still would've found yourself in the lifestyle? Would Ian have felt as great a need to introduce you to it? And if you had gone to college, rather than the military, what would your role at Trident be?

Devon: Um, wow, good questions! I'm not sure if I'd be in the lifestyle if things had been different. Everyone has those moments in their lives that define their future. If I wasn't trying to deal with my grief over John's death, I may not have had the need to gain control over parts of my life, as I did back then. I was on my own downward spiral of destruction after he died. I was taking risks I wouldn't have if I'd been thinking straight. Thankfully, Ian recognized I was beating myself up over the fact I hadn't seen what John was doing to himself. As for college versus the Navy, I don't think I'd be with Trident at all. My dad would probably be grooming me to take the helm of his company when he retires.

Keru K: Ian, are you looking forward to parenthood and what do you think will be the most difficult challenge you, personally, will face?

Ian: Looking forward to parenthood? Abso-fucking-lutely! Before I met my Angel, I hadn't thought I'd ever have kids. What's my most difficult challenge? I really have to stop cursing. I've tossed half a fortune in the swear jar already. Unfortunately, it hasn't helped. Harper's pissed at me because Mara's new favorite word is "twat."

Harper: The only thing funny about that is she only says it when you're around. I'm waiting for her to start calling you Uncle Twat!

Mary D.: Kristen, what do you think of your "Ninja-girl" moniker, and who is your favorite girlfriend so far?

Kristen: I'm actually kind of proud of my nickname. It was a little embarrassing at first, but then I realized the Sexy Six-Pack used it because they respected me for standing up for Colleen. As for my favorite girlfriend, I really can't choose. I love them all so much, but Angie is like the sister I never had.

Chris D.: Mitch, how difficult is it working with family in such an intense business?

Mitch: It has its challenges sometimes, especially when the backlash of that business comes knocking at our gate, and we have to shut the club down for the safety of our members. Thankfully, that hasn't happened often. I'm confident my cousins and their teams are the best at what they do. There have been many times I'm glad I didn't go the military route. Crawling around in mud and muck for days in third-world countries? No, thanks. I'll take my nice, cushy office and leave the rest to them. But don't think for a minute I can't and won't protect my subs, family, friends, and members. My cousins have taught me a lot of what they know.

Kathy G.: This is for Ian, but everyone is welcome to jump in. In this day and age, no one is truly safe anywhere. Will you be training the Trident children in self-defense? How soon would that start and what kind of training would you give them?

    Marco: Before Boss-man answers, let me just say that I'll be training Mara how to defend herself, from the earliest age possible.

    Ian: Amen to that. My kid or kids will know how to kick some serious ass if anyone tries to fuck with them. Boys or girls, they'll know how to fend off an attack, how to shoot, and how to escape from kidnappers if necessary.

Carol M.: Mistress China, this is for you—now that you've found that special guy, what does the future hold for you two?

    Mistress China: Things are going very well for Michael and me, but we're still taking things one day at a time. Yes, we've talked about the future, but, for now, we're keeping our dreams between the two of us. We're still learning about each other and aren't going to rush into marriage or children just yet.

Leia M.: My next question is for Doug and Jenn. How scared are you two of Jenn's uncles when it comes to your feelings for one another?

Doug: Huh? Um, what are you talking about? Jenn and I are just friends. She's too young for me.

Jenn: Too young my ass! I'm twenty-two, an adult!

Ian: Wait! What? What relationship?

Carter: Oh, this is going to be good! Someone get me a beer.

Jake: Excuse me?

Nick: Uh-oh. Can I go get some popcorn before you kill him?

Boomer: Did I miss something here?

Brody: What the fuck?

Doug: Don't look at me! I don't know what they're talking about! Jenn and I don't have a relationship!

Marco: You better not have a relationship with Baby-girl.

Jenn: Everyone, stop! We don't have a relationship. But if we did, I'm an adult, so it's none of your business!

Doug: Except for mine. I mean . . . shit, I'll just shut up now before Ian shoots me.

Devon: A bullet is too good for you. A long slow

death is in your future, Bullseye, if you even think about messing with Jenn.

Jenn: Oh, jeez. Enough already. Aunt Kristen, Aunt Angie, Charlotte, help me, please!

Mistress China: All right, let's table this discussion for now. In front of these nice people asking us questions is not the time to get into this. I'm sorry, everyone. Samantha, can you please have someone ask another question before there's bloodshed?

Nick: Damn, it was just getting good.

Mistress China, Ian, Devon, and Jake: Shut up, Nick.

Nick: Shutting up.

Samantha: Ooooo-kay, moving right along. Does anyone have any more questions? Oh, good.

Anne D.: This is for Boomer and Kat—the others are having babies, but you don't seem to be following this trend. Is it an age thing, since Boomer's the youngest? Eileen had difficulty getting and staying pregnant; I just wondered if history might repeat itself there?

Kat: Hi, Anne! Thanks for asking—and moving things in a different direction before all hell broke loose. Ben and I haven't exactly been trying, but we also haven't been taking precautions. My mother-in-law assures me her difficulty getting pregnant was due to her body and not Rick's. So, hopefully, Ben and I won't have any trouble. For now, we're enjoying our still-newlyweds status. If it happens, it happens.

Kathy G.: Kristen, how many books have you written based on the team and do you plan to write more?

Kristen: While Devon has been my muse for some scenes, the characters I've been writing about have been with me since before I met the Sexy Six-Pack. That said, I do have some new military-type characters, who have been flooding my mind lately, so I might start a new series soon!

Joan T.: For Brody—I know you're from a big family. It didn't take long for Fancy to get pregnant—how many kids will you have? Would you like to equal/beat your mum and dad's record?

Brody: Damn straight it didn't take long for me to get my Fancy-girl pregnant! I've got super sperm! On a serious note, though, I would love to have a big family, as many as we can have. If we beat my folks, great! But if we don't, I'm still good with that. We'll see what happens after this one is born and how much sleep we get before starting on baby number two.

Terry K.: For Fancy—how are your relationships with your dad and half sisters going?

Fancy: Hi, Terry! Things are going okay, I guess. My dad and I talk about once every week or two. He's excited about becoming a grandfather this time around since he's never met my brother's two kids. That's still a work in progress over there, and it's between the two of them. I won't push my brother into a relationship he's not ready to have. As for Natalie, she's been great! We email and chat on the phone a lot, and I think she might be coming to visit in a few weeks before school starts again. I think my dad has put his foot down and convinced my step-mother to let my sister come. We'll see! I still haven't spoken to my youngest sister, yet, and that's okay. Maybe when she's a little older, she'll change her mind.

Anne D.: This is for Kristen's cousin, Will. You looked into the lifestyle after Kristen and Devon hooked up; have you decided it's not for you?

Will: Hi, love! Yes, I did decide it's not for me. I'm a little too set in my ways and too opinionated to submit to someone, and I'm definitely not a Dom. However, I'm in a new relationship and think he may be *the one*! Keeping my fingers crossed it's not just a dream! Smooches!

Terry K.: For the Sexy Six-Pack and spouses—will you ever tell your children about being in the life-style? And for Ian, Angie, Devon, and Kristen, living so close the club, how will you keep your children from learning about the club before you're ready to tell them?

Angie: We've agreed to not be too open about the

lifestyle until it's time to have "the talk" with our kids. Then, we'll explain there are different relationships, and as long as they're healthy ones, there isn't anything wrong with them. We'll see, though, because every time I bring it up, Ian pales and just nods his head. So when I said, "we've agreed," that's what I meant.

Devon: We're going to educate them when they're old enough, but trust me, my kids will not want to see me in the club any more than I'll want to see them! If they're interested, when they're adults, I'll guide them to a different club where I'll know they'll learn about the lifestyle safely.

Leia M.: This is for all the parents and parents-to-be —where are all your kids going to go to school? Public, private, or home schooling?

Kristen: I took a quick consensus, and it looks like everyone is going with public school. We all went that route as kids. If problems arise with that, we'll look at the alternatives.

Tawnya W.: Jen, how do you think your uncles are adjusting to married life?

Jenn: I think they're all doing great. I always knew they'd make good husbands and dads. The only thing that still seems like an issue, though, is the swear jar keeps getting filled.

Terry K.: For Tori, Tyler, and Mitch, any future plans to have any children?

Tori: We're trying!

Tyler: Well, that was short and to the point, sweetheart.

Tori: Fine, what would you add?

Mitch: That we're having a helluva lot of fun while trying.

Tyler: What he said.

Mitch: Actually, we're just not taking any precautions, but if it happens before our wedding next spring, then we're all okay with it.

Tori: Says the man who won't have to squeeze a belly bump into a wedding dress. I told you, if I get pregnant before Christmas, we're eloping. We can do the big party after the baby is born.

Mitch and Tyler: *Yes, dear.*

Tori: That's sarcasm, folks, in case you didn't notice.

Tawnya W: Tori, how many kids do you want?

Tori: We've talked about this at length. While I would love a huge family, Mitch and Ty want three or four max, but we'll take as many as fate allows us.

Anne D.: Roxy and Kayla—we've asked almost everyone else (except Beau and FUBAR lol) whether they're procreating! How do you two feel? I think there's a human urge to have children, but lots of people don't have it, which is totally cool, but you two would make awesome parents—although, let's hope they behave more like Roxy and less like you, Kayla!

Roxy: Bratty sub. Just kidding (well, not really). Anyway, you'll be happy to hear Kayla and I started the process to have children. We've asked a male friend of ours to be the donor. Kayla will be carrying our child, and we plan to go through with everything in the New Year.

Terry K.: For Dakota and Logan—how are you handling everything that y'all went through?

Dakota: Logan's on a case right now and couldn't be here today, so I'll answer for both of us. We're doing well. We're seeing Dr. Trudy Dunbar, together and separately, and she's helping us deal with the trauma we both went through. I think having each other, knowing what the other has been through, has helped us a lot.

Tawnya W.: Mitch, Devon, and Ian—any plans on opening another club on the West Coast? Or anywhere for that matter?

Mitch: We've talked about investing in a second club and have been approached by several people with proposals, but we haven't decided on one yet. Whomever we go into business with will have to be completely vetted, and we have to be sure they'll run the club the same way we run The Covenant.

Terry K.: For Russell—are you enjoying working at Trident Security with Babs? How are things going with Jagger?

Russell: The best thing that has ever happened to me was meeting Senior Chief Evans, although I could have done without getting stabbed. Senior Chief, Lieutenant Sawyer, and everyone else have been awesome, and I can't thank them enough for helping me get Jagger and a place to live and for also giving me a job. As for Babs, I think she's amazing! She's kickass, sarcastic, and funny as hell. However, I wish she'd learn to like some music from the past decade or so. The disco crap has got to go!

Babs: Not a chance, probie. Deal with it. And before anyone asks—he's a good kid, and I like working with him too. FUBAR and Jagger enjoy hanging out with us in the garage all day. They have their own couch, and Beau comes in to visit sometimes.

Robyn G.: A question for Carter—why do you hate your name so much?

Carter: As a kid in school, I was teased, relentlessly, over my name. I was also named for my maternal grandfather. Not sure why, since he kicked my mother out of his house when she got pregnant with me. At least she was in her late teens when she was abandoned. I wish I could say the same for when she abandoned me.

Tawnya W.: Jen, have you read Kristen's BDSM series? If so, how has it changed your view on the lifestyle or did it change your view?

Jenn: LOL! Actually, I'd read a few mild BDSM romances after Uncle Ian and Uncle Devon told me there was a club at the compound. I told them after I started reading Aunt Kristen's BDSM books. My folks had always raised me to be open-minded. I think they knew someday I'd learn about my uncles being in the lifestyle. While it's not something I'm drawn to, I do think if everything is safe, sane, and consensual, there's no problem with it.

Terry K.: For any of the Trident ladies—what is a typical day like for you?

Kristen: Busy, busy, busy!!!! I have a deadline coming up. But I like living in the compound because if JD isn't sleeping well or Devon is away on an assignment, I have plenty of people to help me. The cottage that now houses my writing area and Angie's art studio is fantastic! Sometimes we're there together, working on our individual stuff, and other times I'm by myself—well, not exactly, since JD and Beau are with me.

Anne D.: This is for Master Carl—how are you doing after being accused of being the Kink Killer? Are you still with the submissive you wouldn't name? Are you watching the other Doms find HEAs and hoping for your own?

Master Carl: Thank you for asking, little one. I've been doing well since I was cleared of all suspicion. Somehow, I'm sure it was Ian or Brody's doing, but my name was never released to the press, so my academic reputation is still intact. As for my alibi, I still will not reveal any names. It's a D/s relationship only, and I'm currently not romantically involved with anyone. I'm not sure I'm cut out for a happily ever after, but who knows what the future holds.

Leia M.: This is for Tiny—if you find the right person will you be tempted to go into the lifestyle?

Tiny: Hi, Miss Leia! There's nothing wrong with the lifestyle, but I just don't feel like that's where I'm meant to be on a personal-relationship level. But as they always say, never say never. A good relationship is all about compromise, so I'll cross that bridge if I come to it.

Keru K.: For Darius—within days of you joining Trident you were under a porch, helping to disarm a bomb. Then when Ian dropped the Omega Team in the mountains, you ended up hunting criminals. Are all missions that hectic and unexpected or do they sometimes go as planned? What do you do in your downtime? How is your adjustment from military to civilian life going?

Darius: Thankfully, not all missions are that hectic—although, I'm still not convinced Boss-man doesn't do his best to throw a wrench into things every now and then just for the fun of it. I'm adjusting to civilian life pretty well. Working for TS is like having the best of both worlds—adrenaline rushes and plenty of downtime in between. Right now, though, I'm in South America doing an undercover gig—and wishing I could beat the crap out of these bastards—so I haven't had much downtime. But when I'm in the States, skydiving, climbing, windsurfing, and stuff like that is how I like to relax.

Cheryl M.: So, Ian, what do you see in the future of your work?

Ian: Blowing shit up! Just kidding. TS will continue to grow, but with Angie's due date approaching, I think I'm going to start taking a backseat to my teams. I'm forty-one now and starting to feel it. One word out of you, Egghead, and you'll be on my twat roster for the next year. Same goes for you, Nick.

Nick: Everyone's spoiling my fun today.

Boomer: Um, twat roster?

Ian: Some people have shit lists, I have a twat roster.

Leia M.: Where do you see yourselves being when you guys retire?

Brody: Who's talking about retiring? Boss-man? Figures! He's an old fart! Hmm? What can I change his ring tone to now? How about "When I'm Sixty-Four" by the Beatles?

Ian: What did I just say? Fancy, say goodbye to your Dom for a while. He's going to the Antarctic.

Fancy: Since I'm pregnant, I'm going to resort to bribery. Let him stay here, and I'll make pecan rolls every other day instead of twice a week.

Ian: Every other day? With extra caramel?

Fancy: Yes, with extra caramel.

Ian: Deal. At least until he pisses me off again.

Boomer: That'll be tomorrow.

Lucy T. Do any of you have phobias?

Kristen: Spiders.

Angie: Falling from heights—which is weird since I can look down from them without a problem. Just don't let the elevator lurch downward when I'm on it.

Ian: She screams when that happens.

Angie: Okay, tough man, tell them your phobia.

Ian: I don't have any.

Brody: *Cough* Bullshit.

Nick: Big brother is afraid of—

Ian: Shut up, Nick.

Nick: Lice.

Brody: Bwahahahhahahahahha—he just shuddered, for those of you who can't see him.

Ian: They're disgusting. By the way, Brody's phobias now include lightening and Tasers—

Brody: You get electrocuted and then tell me how much *you* like them.

Ian: And Nick's phobia is clowns.

Nick: I blame that on you, Dev, and John, dressing up as freaky clowns from horror movies for Halloween when I was four. You all laughed your asses off while scaring the crap out of me.

Devon: He peed his pants.

Nick: I was four! Whatever. Next question, anyone, please!

Rhonda B.: This is for Tori's cousin Tiffany—Did you ever call the Dom that Master Mitch asked you to connect with when he was in Vegas for the wedding?

Tiffany: Hi, Rhonda! Yes, I did! Master Cordell and I are getting along well, and I think we're going to be visiting everyone in Florida in the New Year. He's really nice and is helping me recover from my bad experience. I can't thank Master Mitch enough for all he's done.

Mitch: It was my pleasure, Tiffany, and you know you're welcome to come visit any time you want.

Tiffany: Thank you. I can't wait to see the inside of The Covenant. The way Tori describes it, it sounds amazing.

Tori: Trust me, you'll love it!

Jennifer S.: For Marco—now that you have one child, do you want any more?

Marco: My sister, Nina, is probably laughing her ass off in the great beyond, but, yeah, I do. I love my daughter more than I ever knew was possible and would love for her to have a brother or sister someday.

Carrie M.: This is for Colleen—what's it like working for Trident?

Colleen: Oh, good! I get to answer one, lol! I freaking love working for Trident Security. In the beginning, I was so nervous working for six Doms that saw me half-naked all the time at the club, but, as Kristen calls them, the Sexy Six-Pack have been amazing. But, now, not only have they made me feel comfortable working there, but they've also trained me to defend myself. With Reggie's permission, I now have a concealed-carry license (which has already come in handy if you've read Mistress China and Mike's story). My confidence has soared since working here and I no longer take crap from anyone —well, outside of the club where I still have to be submissive lol. My family has issues with me working there, but that's a whole other story. As long as Reggie is okay with it, then I'll be working there as long as Ian, Devon, and everyone else wants me there. It makes me feel great when they all tell me the office would fall apart if I left them.

Ginny P.: Curt, how will you handle it if one of the kids decides to go into the BDSM lifestyle?

Curt: Oh, jeez. Um, well, okay—here I go getting all chauvinistic for a moment. If the boys want to get into it, I'll have them talk to their uncles at Trident about it. As for the girls, they're not going to be dating or having sex until after I'm dead and buried, so that's not a problem. But, honestly, I've been to the club in the past for parties and stuff—because of my close friendship with the team I've been cleared to be there, just not to play—and I understand it more than a lot of non-lifestyle participants. As long as everyone follows the lifestyle mantra—safe, sane, and consensual—then all's good. To each their own. Now, excuse me, while I go scrub the image of any of the kids having sex from my brain.

Aimee A.: Devon, Ian, or Nick, do y'all ever visit John's grave? If so, what's brought you there? And have any of your spouses gone with you?

Devon: Wow, thanks, Aimee, for thinking of John. We know he tends to get lost in the past sometimes. We go to the cemetery all the time to visit him whenever we're in Charlotte where he's buried. It's an almost automatic thing for me. Within twenty-four hours of getting into town, I'll go visit him and talk for a while. We had a stone bench put in at the foot of his grave. I sit there and bring him up to speed with what's going on with all of us. And, yes, Kristen, Angie, and Jake have all gone with us at one time or another. In fact, we'll be taking JD with us next time to introduce him to his namesake.

Ian: Even after all these years, the pain of John's death still hits me hard. I'll never forget how I was called into my captain's office, overseas, and was told what'd happened. I thought it was a sick joke. Once I got my dad on the phone and found out John was really gone, I couldn't get home fast enough. Honestly, there are days when I still curse him for not coming to me and telling me he had a problem. He hid it well. But going to the cemetery, and sitting there for a bit, reminds me of the good times we had growing up.

Nick: I was only eight when John died, so I have a hard time remembering him sometimes—thank God our folks took lots of pictures and videos of us growing up. But going to the cemetery makes me feel closer to him. I always make sure I find a small, cool-looking rock to leave on his headstone before I go there. Just a little sign I was there and that he's loved.

Linda L.: Jenn, what are your plans after college?

Jenn: Hi, Linda! I have one more semester to go —I'm graduating with my bachelor's degree in soci-ology a semester early since I took classes over the summer and winter recesses. Then I'm going to start working on my master's degree in social work. Uncle Ian convinced me to use some of my savings from my parents' life insurance and the sale of our house in Virginia and continue my internship instead of working. I didn't need to work when I moved down here, but I wanted to save that money for when I really needed it—to pay for college and maybe buy a house someday. Working also kept me busy enough to help deal with my parents' murders. Uncle Ian has always said he'd give me spending money and pay for whatever I needed, but I like Grandpa Chuck's ethics—Ian, Devon, and Nick all had to work hard to earn access their trust funds, because nothing worth having in life is easy. I don't want anything handed to me because of my relationship with Uncle Ian and my other uncles. I want to earn what's mine.

Aimee A.: Carter, how's your nephew doing since his surgery?

Carter: Justin's doing well— his body shows no sign of rejecting the kidney. He's back at the University of Montana, trying to catch up on the classes he missed. He's going for pre-med and plans to go to medical school, specializing in pediatric cancer and other diseases.

Rhonda B.: This is for any of the ladies—do you ever do anything just to get a punishment?

Harper, Shelby, Angie, Tori, and Kayla: All the time!

Harper: In my case, because I'm a bit of a pain slut.

Kayla: In my case, because I'm a huge pain slut!

Jordyn: I don't do anything with the intent of getting a punishment out of it, but a lot of the stuff I do has that as the end result. My sarcasm gets me in trouble a lot.

Nick: I'm not one of the ladies, but I can still

answer this—yes! Who knew getting punished could be so much fun?

Brody: Jake, if he's enjoying it, you're not doing it right.

Jake: I'll get right on fixing that.

Riet S. Will, is your story going to be put into a book?

Will: Samantha leaves it up to us if and when we want our stories told. As of right now, I've decided not to go that route, however, that may change in the future. I'm a bit of a private person, so I'm not too comfortable having my story out there.

Aimee A.: Tiny, have any of the ladies tried to set you up on a date?

Tiny: Oh, yes, they have, Miss Aimee! I've met a few of them, but none panned out into a relationship. I was dating someone a while back, but it kind of fizzled. I've asked the ladies not to try to fix me up with anyone right now because I do have my eye on a fine woman. But she's out of state on business, and will be for a while, so I have to wait for her to come back before I can express my interest.

Kimberly M.: How is Master Thomas doing? The Dom who lost a sub to the Kink Killer, after just getting back into the lifestyle after his fiancée's death.

Ian: I wish I could say Master Thomas was doing

well, but I haven't seen him in a while. He hasn't come back to the club since that night.

Mitch: He's not doing well at all. I spoke to him a few weeks ago—we ran into each other at Home Depot. He hasn't gone to any club since Naomi's death, nor has he dated. According to him, he's cursed—first his fiancée was killed in a car accident and then Naomi was murdered. He's seeing a therapist but has pretty much thrown himself into his work.

Rhonda B.: For any of the Doms: have you ever punished your sub and then realized you'd made a HUGE mistake? If so, what did you do?

Ian: I never make mistakes.

Carter: Me either.

Boomer: Same goes for me.

Brody: Me too.

Gray: Same for—

Jordyn: Oh, for fuck's sake. Ask another question because none of them will admit to that.

Carter: That just earned you another half hour with the ball gag.

Nancy L.: For any of the Doms—can you describe your very first scene/intro to BDSM and what you were feeling?

Boomer: It was fucked up and totally awkward— and anyone who tells you differently is lying. Any Dom who wants to be worthy of someone's submission should first learn how to submit before learning how to dominate. I won't describe my first intro scene since I was the one submitting—I'd rather not remember it, thank you—but my first scene as a Dominant was a semi-private one. I'd done practice scenes with subs in the intro classes I'd taken at the time, but doing your first real scene is like someone's taken the training wheels off your bike before you're a hundred percent certain you're ready for it. Plus you have an audience. I was using a crop and was nervous as hell. I was so afraid I was going to hurt the sub that I held back far more than I should have. She never even got into subspace—well, at least not until my mentor stepped in. I felt like a damn fifteen-year-old virgin all over again. While I obviously got better at scening, each time I try a new type of play, a bit of that nervousness comes back. Finding that fine line between giving a sub what they need and going too far and hurting them—physically or mentally—takes a lot of training and experience.

Samantha R.: Jake and Nick—was it love at first sight for either of you?

Nick: Love at first sight? No. Lust at first sight when I first saw him after several years, definitely.

Jake: I'd have to say the same.

DeAnne T.: For the Doms—how hard was it learning to balance what you want and what your sub needs?

Mitch: It's not something you learn overnight,

which is why at The Covenant we insist new Doms take classes on every type of play. They cannot be signed off on play without experiencing that type of play from a submissive's point of view and understanding the mental and emotional process a person goes through when submitting to another person. Doms new to the lifestyle are also hooked up with an experienced Master to apprentice under for three months after finishing their classes. Learning how to find that balance between you and your sub requires several things—among them are compatible limit lists, trust, and an understanding of why you're both in the lifestyle in the first place and what you expect to get out of it.

Rhonda W.: Ian & Angie, is James still a possible name for a baby boy?

Ian: No, it's—

Angie: Yes, it is.

Ian: I thought you changed your mind, Angel.

Angie: I changed it back again.

Ian: Dev, did Kristen drive you this nuts when she was pregnant?

Devon: You have no idea, brother.

Kristen: I did not!

Devon: Yes, you did, Pet. Remember sending me out to the store, three times in one night, because you changed your mind about what ice cream you were craving?

Kristen: That was JD's fault. How was I supposed

to know he didn't like nuts? It wasn't like he could actually tell me from the womb.

Joan T: This is for all the men—what is your favorite "asset" about your significant other.

    Shelby: Oh, boy, this should be interesting.

    Parker: I love her personality more than anything, but she's also got a luscious body.

    Shelby: Good answer, Sir.

    Marco: My beautiful butterfly already knows I love her tits.

    Harper: He worships and tortures them all the time.

    Devon: Kristen's eyes—they were the first things I noticed about her.

    Kristen: Seriously?

    Devon: Yup—then your tits. That's five for rolling your eyes, Pet.

    Kristen: Ugh—yes, Sir.

    Ian: Every inch of my Angel from head to toe.

    Angie: Aw, thanks, honey.

    Boomer: Kat's ass. I love it.

    Jake: Nick's eyes.

    Nick: Jake's back and shoulders.

    Brody: Fancy's baby-bump.

    Mitch and Tyler: Tori's ass.

    Mitch: And Ty's ass too.

    Remi: Abigail's legs—especially in thigh highs.

    Gray: For me, it's her tits. I love playing with them.

Curt: All of Dana's curves.

Carter: The fact that Jordyn can kick ass and her sarcasm. I love how her mind works too. Oh, and her pussy. Can't forget that.

Jordyn: You better not forget that.

Jase: Brie's mouth. I can kiss her all day.

Mike: I love Charlotte's legs—especially when she's in heels—and her long hair.

Charlotte: My hair?

Mike: Yup, I love when you let me brush it out. It's super silky. I love the feel of it.

Charlotte: Hmm. I'll have to remember that, Michael.

Samantha: Any more questions? No? Well, then I thank you all for participating! I hope everyone had a good time.

PART FOUR
SHORT STORIES

***Please note there are spoilers within these short stories for books released prior to November 11, 2018.

CHRISTMAS IN CUFFS
JAKE & NICK

Throwing his canvas duffel bag in the back of his truck, Nick Sawyer waved goodbye to the other members of SEAL Team Three and climbed into the driver's seat. They were all hurrying home to surprise their loved ones for Christmas. Their OCONUS mission had ended earlier than expected, and if traffic was on his side, he'd be walking into his condo and Jake Donovan's arms at just before midnight. He was already getting hard wondering what his boyfriend would come up with to celebrate.

This was the second and last Christmas they'd be having in San Diego. Next year, they'd be in Tampa with Nick's brothers, Jake's employers at Trident Security. Ian and Devon Sawyer had been surprised yet supportive when their good friend and teammate had fallen in love with their younger brother. Not only was Jake his lover, but he was also his Dom. Finding out he was a sexual submissive had shocked the shit out of Nick, but he was fine with it as long as Jake was the man dominating him.

The last time Nick had spoken to Jake was ten days ago. At that time, they'd made plans to celebrate Christmas two days late. He'd already gotten Jake a present before being deployed two months ago, not knowing when he'd get another chance to do it. It had been sitting in his locker on the base all this time, and he'd grabbed it before hightailing it to the parking lot.

Tomorrow, they'd get on Skype and call Nick's growing family and Jake's mother and brother in Tampa to wish everyone a great day. He was dying to see how big little JD was getting. Devon and his wife Kristen had given Chuck and Marie their first grandchild back in September. A few weeks after that, the Sawyer clan had gathered in Tampa for Ian and Angie's wedding. Wondering when the newlyweds would be starting a family shifted to him and Jake. Did Jake want kids? And, hell, did Nick want kids? He'd never thought about it before. What the hell would two Navy SEALs turned private security operatives know about raising kids?

Maybe they'd talk about having kids someday but not yet. Once he retired from the Navy in five months and moved to Tampa, he'd broach the subject with Jake. Now wasn't a good time. The man had plenty to deal with. For the past year, he'd been hiring and training the west coast Trident Security team. Before he and Nick left for Florida, Jake had to make a decision about who to put in charge of the team. There were seven men and one woman, and they were all leader material. Jake, Devon, and Ian had wanted the cream of the crop for the new team and had chosen well from a list of candidates—some from the military and others from law enforcement.

Pulling into the parking lot of their condo complex, Nick shifted his hips, trying to give his throbbing cock some room in his tactical pants. He parked, jumped out, and grabbed his duffel, praying Jake was still awake. Or maybe it would be better if he wasn't. Nick enjoyed watching his lover sleep—especially since he'd finally let his traumatic senior year in high school stay in the past where it belonged. Since they'd moved in together, Jake no longer hid his scars under a T-shirt at night. In fact, massaging his Dom's bare back was one of Nick's favorite things to do when they were relaxing at home. Of course that usually led to more of his other favorite things to do.

Putting the key in the front door lock, Nick quietly let himself into the foyer and shut the door behind him. A soft glow from under the microwave came from the kitchen to his right, while another one came from the living room. That one flickered, and Nick figured it was from the gas fireplace.

He knew better than to step into the living room without announcing himself. Once a SEAL, always a SEAL, and Nick might end up staring down the barrel of one of Jake's guns if he wasn't careful.

Leaving his duffel on the foyer floor, he took one step and whispered, "Sir?"

A *thunk* on a table, which was probably a now discarded weapon, was followed by Jake pivoting around the corner, his eyes wide in a combination of surprise, love, and lust. God, the man was beautiful. Six foot five and two-hundred-ten pounds of solid muscle that was only covered by a pair of lightweight, cotton sweatpants. Nick's mouth watered at the sight of every hard mesa and valley of the man's torso. The growing bulge below that was just as tempting.

Jake didn't say a word, but strode forward and kept coming, pinning Nick against the wall. His hands cupped Nick's whiskered jaw, and his head descended until their lips met. The kiss was far from gentle, both giving what the other wanted and taking what each offered. It had been far too long for both of them. "Hi, honey, I'm home" could wait until after they had an orgasm or two . . . or three.

Jake's hands slid down Nick's neck and grasped the edge of his T-shirt. With one smooth yank, the fabric was ripped in two. Nick's heart pounded wildly. They were skin to skin for the first time in eight weeks, and it felt incredible. As much as he wanted it to continue, though, he needed to clean up. He hadn't wanted to delay seeing Jake long enough to take a shower at the base, but now that they were together, he really needed a few minutes with some hot water and soap.

When Jake's mouth left his and dropped to his neck, Nick rasped, "S-Sir. I need a shower before we go further."

Jake licked his ear. "Showering with my subbie sounds like a great start to a welcome home celebration. Let's go."

Following Jake, Nick stopped short in the living room, his jaw almost hitting the floor. The flickering lights he'd assumed were from the gas fireplace were from the glow of a Christmas tree. The seven-foot balsam fir was in the corner of the room with hundreds of twinkling lights and a star on top. He couldn't believe Jake had done this. Last year, Nick had needed to beg and barter before dragging his Dom to get a tree. Christmas had always been the youngest Sawyer brother's favorite time of the year, and no matter where he was on that day, he'd found some way to celebrate, whether big or small. Jake on the other hand, had only done the very bare basics for the holiday, if he'd even done that.

"You—you got a tree?" *Yeah, there you go, stating the obvious.* His gaze fell to the fireplace. Two red and white holiday stockings hung from the mantle, one with Jake's name, one with his.

Jake shrugged then took Nick's hand and pulled him toward their bedroom and shower. "I know how much it means to you, so I wanted it up before you got home. I actually just finished putting the ornaments on this afternoon."

In the master bath, Jake flipped on the water in the shower to warm it up as Nick stripped out of his pants, boots, and what remained of his torn shirt. Stepping under the spray, he felt the last of the stressful mission leave his body along with the accompanying grime and sweat. He rested his hands on the tiled wall in front of him and dipped his head, letting the water pelt his shoulders and neck. Jake stepped in behind him, now gloriously naked, and grabbed a loofah and the Dolce & Gabbana body wash they both favored. Slowly and sensually, Jake cleaned his sub, and, once more, Nick thanked God for bringing this man into his life. He would never love another as much as he loved Jake.

The sudsy loofah didn't miss a single inch of Nick's body, including his prominent hard-on which grew in intensity with every stroke of the raspy material. After he was all soaped up, Jake removed the showerhead from its perch and rinsed the lather from Nick's skin.

Feeling rejuvenated, Nick turned around and met Jake's

green-eyed, lust-filled gaze with his own blue one. "What would my Sir like me to do?"

Reaching around him, Jake turned off the water. "Grab a towel, razor, and shaving cream, while I go get a bowl for water. I'm getting rid of that scruff of yours before we go any further."

Nick's eyes and lust flared. It wouldn't be the first time Jake had shaved him, and damn, if it wasn't one incredible turn on when he did.

Minutes later, Nick was flat on his back on the bed. One towel was underneath him and another lay across his chest. A bowl of water sat on the night stand. Jake straddled his hips and spread shaving cream over Nick's jaw, cheeks, chin, and upper lip. His Dom seemed oblivious to the hard cock pressing against his ass cheeks, but Nick knew better and wondered what their first scene of the evening would be. Whatever it was, he was sure to enjoy every minute of it—at least, the last few minutes of it. Sometimes Jake used the bullwhip on his subbie's back and ass. While the first strikes always seemed to be the worst, Nick would soon be in subspace as the pain morphed into pleasure. By the time he was allowed to come, he'd be begging for it. The orgasms he had after a whipping were beyond explosive and comprehension. Now, just the thought of a whipping had Nick needing relief—but all in due time.

The razor rasped across his skin as stroke by stroke Jake removed the coarse whiskers. Nick had shaved earlier in the week because the team had used smoke grenades during a raid. Beards interfered with the masks they'd needed to wear to breathe. The edges of the masks wouldn't seal properly unless they were against bare skin.

The repeated motions of the razor stroke followed by Jake rinsing the blade off in the water had Nick's eyes growing heavy, but he loved watching his Dom perform this act, so he forced them to stay open.

Jake dragged the blade up under Nick's chin. "Everyone come home okay, Junior?"

"Yeah. A few bumps and bruises but nothing that required stitches or casts."

"Always a good thing." That was all Jake could and would ask about Nick's mission. Despite being a former SEAL and now working for a security company that had many government contracts and a high clearance level, Jake couldn't know the details of Nick's missions. Most of them were classified and the specifics were imparted on a need to know basis. If a person didn't need to know, then they didn't get to know. It was one of the reasons many SEAL marriages and relationships failed. But in Nick's case, Jake understood better than any other SEAL's significant other and that helped a lot.

When his sub's face was finally whisker free, Jake tossed the razor into the bowl. Taking the towel from Nick's chest, he wiped the last of the shaving cream from his face.

The Dom climbed off Nick and the bed. "I have to get something. Present for me."

As Jake strode from the room, Nick stood and opened the drawer to his night stand. Pulling out the collar Jake had given him last year, he put it on as he dropped to his knees beside the bed. Most people would see it as a man's silver necklace with what appeared to be a charm similar to a yin-yang. But the black onyx and silver pendant was a BDSM symbol. Instead of two halves complementing each other, this had three. There were several different meanings for it in the community, but Nick like Jake's the best. The three pieces represented Nick, Jake, and their love and commitment to each other. Nick always wore it unless he was on a mission or it interfered with his Naval dress or duties.

Minutes passed, and by the time Jake reentered the room, Nick was in full presentation mode. Knees shoulder width apart, head bowed in respect, hands behind him in the at ease position. Jake's bare feet stopped in front of him. "Look at me, Junior."

Nick raised his chin until his gaze met Jake's devilish one. From the man's finger hung a pair of leather cuffs. Licking his lips, Nick swallowed hard. The last time Jake had used those, he'd given Nick the longest and best blowjob of his lifetime. When he'd finally been allowed to come, he'd almost passed out from the intensity.

"Can you handle this right now?"

He knew what Jake was asking. Did he want to say his safeword? Hell no!

"Yes, Sir."

"Good. Come with me."

Standing, Nick followed Jake out the door in confusion. They weren't doing this in bed? Once more, he stopped short in the living room. Jake had opened the pullout couch and turned off the table lamp that'd been on. The only light in the room came from the Christmas tree. They were going to scene under its twinkling branches and star. And Jake thought he couldn't think of romantic things to surprise Nick with. The man was so wrong.

"Lay down on your back. Hands above your head. Bend your knees."

After Nick did as he was told, Jake attached the cuffs to his wrists and then to the metal bar of the couch's bed. The Dom climbed between Nick's spread legs and opened a tube of lubricant, covering several fingers of one hand with it. "I missed you so much, babe."

"I missed you, too, Sir."

Without another word, Jake made himself comfortable on his stomach, his breath caressing Nick's groin in warm puffs, exciting him even more. Fingers breached the rim of Nick's ass, and he couldn't control the groan of need that escaped him. With each stroke, the fingers advanced, lighting up the nerves inside. "More, Sir. Please."

"Uh-uh, Junior. I've been dreaming of this for weeks. I'm going to take my time and enjoy every minute of it."

"Shit!"

Jake chuckled but followed through with his statement. Torturously slow, he stretched and fucked his lover's ass. His other hand closed around Nick's shaft and pumped it a few times before tilting it toward his mouth. Nick's eyes fluttered shut as warm, moist lips closed around him. He tugged against his restraints in a futile attempt to hold Jake's head where it was. The man's tongue lapped at the vein on the underside of Nick's cock, eliciting a gasp of pleasure.

The combined sensations attacking his ass and dick were too much and yet not enough. Not enough to send him over the edge. Jake alternated between speeding up and slowing down. His tongue swirled around the tip before taking Nick deeply again and again. He caressed Nick's balls and moaned around him, sending vibrations surging through his submissive's body.

Nick fought the urge to shift his hips and beg for more. It'd become a game between the Dom and sub over the past year. How long could Jake torture Nick before he began to plead for release?

Gasps and moans flowed from Nick's lips, but he refused to ask for more beyond his one request moments ago. Through heavy lidded eyes he watched his Dom make love to him. And, yes, it was love. Nick had never truly known that emotion until he'd fallen hard for Jake.

The hand at his balls moved upward, massaging his taut abs and chest. Jake reached up and placed his fingers on Nick's lips. Without hesitation, the sub's tongue lashed out and sucked the digits into his mouth. He nibbled and licked them, wishing they were Jake's cock instead.

Each minute felt like ten. Jake's hand trailed back down to Nick's chest and plucked his peaked nipple. He added a third finger to the ass he was fucking, and Nick saw stars. His head began to spin. A tingling in his spine forewarned his coming orgasm. His breathing and heart rate increased.

The Dom was all too aware of the changes in his submissive's body. He deep-throated him over and over, swallowing hard each time. Nick couldn't take it any longer. "Please, Sir, please let me come. It—it's been too long. I'm going to explode."

Jake released him just long enough to say, "Come for me, Junior."

His warm mouth engulfed Nick's shaft again and every-thing sped up. The fingers in his ass pumped faster and harder. Jake's head bobbed up and down. Nick was beyond able to stop the roaring freight train of release and yelled Jake's name as he shot cum down his lover's throat in streams that didn't want to ebb. Black and white flashes replaced the multi-colored lights of the tree in front of Nick's eyes as Jake swallowed every ounce of his seed. Nick's body shook with the force of it all until it was spent and he had nothing more to give. He collapsed into the mattress as Jake released him and licked his lips in satisfaction.

As Jake got to his knees, Nick's gaze fell to the man's straining erection. "Fuck me, Sir. Let me take care of that for you."

Again without a word, Jake crawled forward and lined his cock up with Nick's ass. The hole was already stretched wide for him, and he had no trouble easing in. Nick smiled as Jake's eyes rolled back into his head in ecstasy.

"Damn, I missed this. So tight. So fucking perfect. I love you, babe."

"Love you, too, Sir. Fuck me as hard as you want. As hard as you need."

With a roar, Jake did just that. His hips pumped piston-like, harder with every thrust. He fucked Nick like his life depended on it, and Nick took everything the man gave him. Bending his knees toward his chest, Nick gave the Dom more room. Jake slid deeper in the ass that hugged him.

"Shit, Junior! Can't—Can't hold back."

"I don't want you to, Sir. Give it to me. All of it."

"Aaaaahhhhhh, fuuuuuuuuuuuck!" Jake emptied himself

into Nick's core, thrusting until he finally collapsed on top of him. The Dom struggled to get oxygen in his lungs while Nick reveled in the weight of his lover.

Pushing himself up on his forearms, Jake kissed Nick's lips. "Welcome home, babe."

"Merry Christmas," he responded with a smile. "Can you release me so I can hold you, Sir, please?"

Rolling off him, Jake reached up and undid the restraints. He rubbed Nick's shoulders and arms, making sure there was good blood flow. Pulling Nick into his arms, Jake cuddled him as they lay under the blinking lights.

How long they stayed like that, Nick wasn't sure, but it was well after midnight, which meant it was Christmas Day. He couldn't wait any longer to give Jake his present.

Pushing up from the mattress, he said, "Be right back." Comfortable in his nakedness, he hurried to the foyer and pulled the wrapped box from his duffel. Suddenly, he was nervous. What would Jake say when he saw it? Only one way to find out.

Climbing back into the pullout bed, he sat, leaning on the back of the couch. He handed Jake the oblong box.

His lover raised an eyebrow and sat up next to him. "What's this?"

"I can't wait until morning. Open it now."

Jake rubbed one eye with the heel of his hand, then began to open the bright wrapping paper. Nick's pulse pounded as butterflies took flight in his stomach. Tossing the wrapping aside, Jake opened the box and shifted through the tissue to find the new KA-BAR knife Nick had gotten him with his initials JRD engraved on the blade. But that's not what had the Dom freezing with his hand in midair. He was staring at the little blue ribbon wrapped around the hilt and the platinum ring attached to it. Also attached to the ribbon was a little note in Nick's handwriting that said, "Marry me?"

Seconds passed as Jake stared at the contents of the box. Finally, he looked at Nick. "Before I answer that, I have present for you too." Leaping from the bed, he stepped over to the fireplace and reached into Nick's stocking. He pulled out a small box and tossed it to Nick, whose mouth fell open. A box this size could only hold one thing.

Jake sat down next to him again, grinning. "Open it, Nick."

Tearing off the red and green paper, he lifted the lid of the box and gaped. The ring was eerily similar to the one he'd picked out for Jake. In fact, it was from the same jeweler.

Jake took Nick's hand, drawing his gaze. "I'll say yes if you do."

THE LOVE YOU GIVE
PARKER & SHELBY

Shelby Christiansen unpacked, then repacked the little, blue knapsack. Full of nervous energy, she tried to get herself under control. Her husband and Dom, Parker, would laugh at her again if he saw her, but he was in the bathroom shaving. He'd taken her mind off today for a little while in the shower by giving her two amazing orgasms before entering her from behind and finding his own release. But now that she was dressed, with nothing left to do but wait, she couldn't sit still.

The door to the bathroom swung open and before she had a chance to hide what she'd been doing, Parker strolled into the room, looking for his shirt. His chest rumbled with a deep chuckle, drawing her gaze to his tan, muscular pecs. Damn, he was beautiful, but she wouldn't tell him that. Like most men, he thought the word was more feminine than masculine. He preferred she use the word handsome.

Parker stepped over to the bed and slid the knapsack from her reach. Sitting, he pulled her between his legs.

"Baby, you know Sister Patrice said we shouldn't bring anything the first time we meet him. We want him to like us, not the toys and stuff we bring. No bribery."

Rubbing his velvety, bare shoulders, she dropped her forehead to his. "I know. But what if he doesn't like us?"

"He will. I promise. What's not to like? He's going to have a beautiful and caring mother and a super cool dad."

"What? I can't be beautiful, caring, *and* super cool?" she teased.

Cupping her jaw, he kissed her sweetly. "You're going to be the best mother there ever was or will be."

What he didn't add was what he'd told her many times before. It's not giving birth to a child that makes you a good mother, it's the love you give that child. Shelby couldn't have children since her first of two battles with cancer had left her barren. After she and Parker had fallen in love and gotten married in Vegas, with their friends surrounding them, they'd looked into adoption. But in the United States, teenage and single mom pregnancies weren't as frowned upon as they'd been years ago, and none of the public adoption agencies would approve the couple due to her health history, even though she was now cancer-free. Turning to private agencies hadn't produced any success either. Nowadays, birth mothers were given thick dossiers on prospective parents and picked the ones they wanted to give their newborns to, and again her cancer had been an issue.

Then, a miracle in the form of Master Carter's submissive, lover, and partner, Jordyn, had stepped forward. Carter was a good friend of the men of Trident Security, a private-sector business run by the Sawyer brothers, who also owned the BDSM club they all belonged to. All Shelby knew about the other couple was they worked for the government. But if she had to guess, it was for the CIA or FBI or some agency like that. In her mind, Carter was like a US version of James Bond—he surely had the looks for the role.

Apparently, the couple had heard about the problems Shelby and Parker were having and had come up with a solution. Jordyn had been born in Argentina and lived there until she was fourteen. Her parents had died, how, Shelby didn't know, and Jordyn had spent three months in Sister Patrice's orphanage, before being brought to the states by an uncle as soon as he'd learned of her whereabouts.

After receiving pictures, videos, and profiles of over two dozen children looking for forever homes, Shelby and Parker had poured through them. She wished she could take them all, but little, six-year-old Franco had won their hearts the moment they watched his video. Bright-eyed and chubby cheeked, he was full of life. From what his profile said, he'd been born to a single mother who'd died when he was four years old from a burst appendix. She hadn't gone to the doctor or hospital because the closest one had been an hour away from her small village, and she hadn't had anyone to leave Franco with. By the time she did try to make the trip, it'd been too late.

Having made their decision, Parker and Shelby had contacted Sister Patrice and arranged to come meet Franco. They'd flown into Buenos Aires yesterday and had checked into the Alvear Palace Hotel, ninety minutes from the orphanage. If all worked out well today, they'd spend the rest of the week before Easter processing the paperwork to adopt the boy. Sister Patrice had a relative in the government who helped move the procedure along. It was all legal, but they would be moved to the top of the court docket, cutting the wait time dramatically.

Jordyn had told them Sister Patrice did her best to find good homes for her charges but was more open to the problems that threw up roadblocks for some prospective parents. Since Shelby was in remission and had gotten a clean bill of health recently, that wasn't an issue this time. Parker had a thriving construction business and had even taken on an old college buddy as a partner to help with the increasing number of contracts, which meant Shelby was able to resign from her job. The choice between being a stay-at-home mom or working in the human resource department for a pharmaceutical company for an obnoxious boss was a no-brainer. Her last day had been four weeks ago, and as soon as they'd let Sister Patrice know their decision, Shelby had been finishing Franco's bedroom and buying him clothes, toys, and everything else the little boy would need.

A knock sounded at the door, and Parker stood and grabbed his blue polo shirt. "Must be the driver and body-guards." Part of the area they had to drive through was not the greatest, and Ian Sawyer had arranged for them to be safe going to and from the orphanage.

Pulling on his shirt, Parker answered the door. There was no disguising the surprise in his voice. "Hey, what are you doing here?"

"We're just here for the food, my friend."

Shelby spun around at the sound of Carter's deep timber as he and Jordyn strode into the room. Throwing her arms open, Shelby hugged Jordyn first and then Carter. Tears filled her eyes, and the Dom pulled back and wiped her cheek with his thumbs. "What's this, little one?"

Embarrassed, she backed up a few steps and waved her hands in front of her face. "Don't mind me. I'm just super nervous."

"She's worried Franco won't like her." Her husband moved behind her and wrapped his arms around her waist. "But I keep telling her that won't happen. So back to my original question, what are you two doing here? Not that I'm not glad to see you."

Striding over to the table and chairs by the window, Jordyn sat down. The dark-haired woman was a knockout, kick-ass, sarcastic, and sweet—Carter had chosen well for his life partner; she kept him on his toes. "We were sort of in the area and figured you could use some support. Besides, it's been a while since I've visited Sister Patrice, and she's been asking to meet Carter."

"So, I'm the one who should be worried about the trip to the orphanage, Shelby," Carter said with a grin. "You, on the other hand, should listen to your Dom. Franco is going to love you, just like everyone else does."

When she'd faced her second battle with cancer, her parents had both passed away a few years earlier, and she'd tried to deal with it herself. That's when Parker had stepped in to help, and the rest, as they say, is history. But when everyone at The Covenant had learned she was sick and undergoing chemo, she'd found out how many friends she truly had. They'd all stepped forward and helped any way they could, but mostly it was their emotional support that had been most appreciated. When she'd shaved her short blonde hair during her chemo, almost all the male members had shaved their heads to boost her spirits, along with a few of the women.

Jordan took a sip of the bottled water she'd brought in with her. "I know you don't have to leave for the orphanage for another hour, so how about going shopping with us really quick? Your bodyguards and driver are downstairs already—we called Ian to find out who he'd contracted. While Parker and Carter load up on some food staples for Sister Patrice, you and I can do some damage in the children's clothing shop. I always bring her clothes, socks, underwear, and sneakers in different sizes, so she has them in stock whenever needed. Sound like a plan? It'll get your mind off worrying."

Relief had Shelby's shoulders relaxing. "That sounds like a great plan. Let me just use the bathroom, and then we're out of here."

Two and a half hours later, the foursome, two bodyguards, and their driver, pulled their vehicles past the wall surrounding the orphanage's courtyard. Carter and Jordyn had followed the others in a rented van filled with all their purchases. There was a small fence blocking off a play area where about thirty children were enjoying themselves under the watchful eye of three women wearing traditional navy and white headpieces, which were in contrast to their jeans and button-down, white, Oxford shirts. One of the nuns waved at the newcomers, then exited the gate separating her from them.

"Jordyn! What a surprise!" The woman, who looked to be

in her sixties, embraced her former charge. "I didn't know you were coming today."

"And miss an opportunity to see you? Never." Jordyn turned to her lover and friends. "Sister Patrice, this is Carter. And this is Shelby and Parker Christiansen, who are very excited to meet their new son."

"Well, I'm very excited to introduce you to Franco," Sister Patrice said, shaking the couple's hands before addressing the taller man with his long, dirty-blond hair pulled back in a ponytail. "So you're Carter, the man with one name who's won my little girl's heart. Treat her right or I'll put in a bad word for you with the man upstairs."

As she pointed to the sky, Carter burst out laughing. "No worries there, Sister. Jordyn will always come before me."

Shelby almost choked on the veiled innuendo, and by the way Parker hid his grin behind his fist, and Jordyn's eyes flaring, they'd noticed it too. But the sexual reference clearly went over the nun's head.

"Well, now that the pleasantries and threats are out of the way, why don't you come inside, and we'll chat for a bit before I introduce you to Franco?"

"Actually," Carter interrupted, "I'll stay here and help bring in the supplies. Where do they go?"

Jordyn held up a finger to him. "Give me one second to fetch Pedro, their handyman, to help, and I'll show you where everything goes. Unless things have change since I was here last."

She raised a questioning eyebrow at the nun, who shook her head. "No, everything is still the same. Pedro is in his workshop. Shelby and Parker can come with me."

The couple followed her into a single-story building, larger than Shelby had expected. "I didn't know you were from America, Sister. If I'm not mistaken, I detect a Chicago accent."

The woman grinned as she held open the door to her sparsely furnished office. "Yes. I was born and raised there. We've had a few missionaries from my childhood parish visiting and helping out for the past two weeks. They come every year, and, every time, my old accent returns for a few weeks. Please, have a seat."

Shelby's nervousness must have been showing as she fingered the D/s collar Parker had given her, because the nun gave her a reassuring smile as she sat behind the desk. "I promise, Shelby, I don't bite or snarl. Please relax."

Taking a deep breath, she let it out slowly as Parker clasped her hand in support. "Sorry. I'm not sure why I'm so edgy."

"It's understandable. It's not every day you meet the boy who will be your son."

Her eyes widened. "H—he's definitely ours?"

Sister Patrice's smile widened. "I wouldn't have had you fly down here to tell you no. With Jordyn's glowing recommendation, your background checks, and the fact you're in remission, I don't see any reason for you not to take Franco home with you after the court proceedings. I've already arranged for you to be on the court docket on Thursday. You'll receive a temporary passport for Franco, his birth certificate, and all the papers you'll need for the US Social Security Administration at that time." She handed Parker a sheet of paper. "Here's a list of things you'll need to do before then, and things you'll need to bring to court. It's the same list I emailed you. One thing you'll want to do right away, because I've had people forget and have to stay an extra day, is to book Franco a seat on the plane."

"That won't be necessary," he explained. "The parents of very good friends of ours have a private jet that flew us down here. We've become close to them, and that was their adoption present to us." Ian and Devon Sawyer's father was a self-made, real estate billionaire, and his wife was a plastic surgeon who spent a lot of time in third-world countries with Operation Smile. As soon as they'd heard about Franco, they'd offered one of Chuck Sawyer's company jets, and Marie Sawyer wouldn't take no for an answer. It'd been awesome taking the long flight in luxurious style—and being inducted into the Mile-High Club.

"Nice friends." After a few more minutes of going over a few things, Sister Patrice stood. "Well, then, let me go get Franco and introduce you. The art room is right across the hall. We'll meet you in there. It's his favorite school subject."

They'd already known that as most of his video had been filmed in that room. For a young child, he was a very talented artist, and Shelby and Parker planned to help him cultivate his gift.

When they stepped into the room, it was just as they'd seen on the video. Long tables and shelves held a variety of artistic mediums from crayons to pastel pencils and paints to clay. All around the room, the children's art projects hung on the walls. Shelby scanned them until she spotted Franco's name at the bottom of several drawings. "Parker, look how he drew this dog! He's going to love Spanky!"

Their lovable and huge Bullmastiff, Spanky, had been adopted by Parker before he and Shelby had gotten together, and as a Dom in the lifestyle, he'd been too amused to change the name the dog had already been dubbed.

Her husband stepped behind her to eye the picture and placed his hands on her hips. "He really is good. I can't draw a stick figure to save my life, which is why I read blueprints and don't draw them."

A noise behind them had the couple turning to see Sister Patrice and a dark-haired, little boy. Shelby recognized her son immediately. Her son. Yes, from the moment she'd seen his video, she'd known he was going to be theirs.

Sister Patrice stood behind Franco, with her hands on his shoulders. She'd explained earlier she'd tell him the news when she thought it was the right time. Since the nun was experienced in the introductions of children and prospective parents, they'd agreed to follow her lead. Being bilingual, Sister Patrice and the other nuns taught the children in both Spanish and English so communicating with new families would be easier. "Franco, this is Mr. and Mrs. Christiansen. They've been admiring your artwork."

The boy smiled shyly, but his dark brown eyes shined with pride. "I like to draw."

Her heart expanding with love, Shelby swallowed hard and sat in a nearby chair, so she was on eye level with the precious, little boy. "You do it very well, Franco. I love your picture of the dog. We have a dog—would you like to see a picture of him?" Franco nodded and stepped closer as Shelby dug in her purse while Parker sat next to her. "See, this is

Spanky. He's a big dog—bigger than you. But he loves little boys and girls, and he's very gentle."

Franco giggled. "He's funny looking."

"Yes, he is," Parker said with a grin. "He's always making silly faces like that."

"I wish I had a dog." The wistfulness in his soft voice was unmistakable.

Her eyes filling with happy tears, which she tried to keep from falling, Shelby looked up at Sister Patrice who nodded and sat down next to the couple, taking the little boy's hand. "Franco, Mr. & Mrs. Christiansen would like to be your parents . . . *tu madre y tu padre*. Would you like that?"

The boy's eyes went wide. "*¿De verdad?*"

"Really. They live in the United States and want you to go live with them and Spanky." She grinned, indicating the photo he was still holding.

As if he still couldn't believe it, he looked back and forth between the adults. Parker held out his hand. "Would you like to come live with us, Franco? We have a nice house that's right near a school and park. There are lots of other children in the neighborhood. And I know Spanky would love to be your dog." His voice grew thick with emotion. "We'd love to be your mother and father."

His mouth open, Franco shook Parker's hand and began to nod his head, but then his eyes furrowed. "But what about Victor? Can he come, too?"

Not knowing who he was talking about, Shelby glanced at Parker and then Sister Patrice. "Who's Victor? I don't remember that name from the profiles you sent."

"He's my best friend," Franco piped up before the nun could speak. "Can you be his mother and father too? Please?"

Sister Patrice had an apologetic expression on her face. "I'm sorry. Like Franco said, the two are fast friends. Victor is also six years old. I didn't send his file to you because, at the time, he had a pending adoption. However, it fell through after I learned from the background checks that the couple had fabricated quite a few things on their application. I thought it was best to deny them and have Victor remain with us."

Shelby was stunned. The hopeful look on Franco's face was more than she could bear, and she turned to see Parker staring at her. There was nothing but love in his eyes as he raised an eyebrow at her. She nodded back. His gaze never left hers as he asked, "Sister Patrice, how hard would it be to add another application to the court docket?" He was purposely being vague in case the answer was not what they wanted Franco to hear.

"Well, since I have connections, it won't be hard at all. Would you like me to go find Victor, so you can meet him?"

Tapping her lap, Shelby beckoned Franco to sit on it. When he did so, with the shyness that had returned, she gently put her arm around him. "Franco, how would you like Victor to be more than your best friend? How would you like him to be your brother?"

He threw his arms around her neck and hugged her tightly. "Yeah!"

———

THREE DAYS LATER, THE NEW FAMILY OF FOUR WAS ON THE PRIVATE jet, soaring at 41,000 feet. Shelby tucked a blanket around Franco's shoulders and then did the same for Victor. After ninety minutes of their first time on an airplane, looking at the clouds, and playing a few games, they'd passed out on opposite sides of one of the couches. For not being blood related, the boys' features were remarkably similar. Being the same age, they'd probably be mistaken for twins until they grew older.

Parker came out of the bathroom and sat down in one of the recliners, pulling Shelby onto his lap. "Come here, little mama."

"Yes, Master Papa," she teased. Setting down the cell phone she'd been using moments before, she cupped his jaw in her hands and pecked his lips with hers. "Kristen said the girls took care of everything. The second twin bed and dresser were delivered this morning, and they made sure there's two of everything the boys will need. Jenn has been showing Spanky the video of the boys we made, so hopefully he'll recognize their voices right away. She's not sure if he understands what he's watching, but she swears he's enjoying it and his tail wags each time she plays it."

"He's going to love the boys."

"Just like we do already. I-I still can't believe we're parents to two boys. I hope we do a good job."

He squeezed his arms around her. "It'll be trial and error and correction, just like everything else in life. If . . . well, I should say *when* we hit a rough spot, because I'm sure we'll hit a lot of them, we'll do the best we can and give them all the love we have."

Leaning forward again, she kissed him deeper this time. While she would love to take it further, they now had young, impressionable boys to think of first, so she reluctantly pulled away and snuggled into his chest, tucking her head under his chin. "I love you, Papa Christiansen."

"And I love you, Mama Christiansen, and I always will."

FANCY MEETING YOU HERE
BRODY & FANCY

Wednesday . . .

Exiting the private jet's lavatory, Brody Evans ducked into the kitchen area and grabbed two bottled waters from the refrigerator before returning to the couch his fiancée was sitting on. He plucked the notepad and pen from her hands and replaced them with one of the bottles. "Drink up, Ms. Fancy Maguire, soon to be Mrs. Fancy Evans, and stop worrying about all the little details. Everything's going to be just fine."

She snorted as she opened the bottle. "Says the man who only needs to make sure his Navy whites are pressed and his shoes are shined."

Plopping down next to her, he tossed the pen and pad into her over-sized purse sitting on the floor by her feet. "I resent that remark. I've got a lot of things to do, mainly making my beautiful fiancée relaxed and happy before making her my wife in three days."

They were on their way to Dallas in the Trident Security jet, with CC Chapman in the pilot's seat. The other occupants included bridesmaids Katerina Michaelson and Harper DeAngelis, whose husbands would be joining them on Friday, the day before the wedding. Kat was reclining in one of the plush, leather chairs, while Harper sat at a table, typing a court brief on her laptop. Brody's niece, Jenn Mullins, and Boomer Michaelson's teenage foster sister, Alyssa Wagner, were entertaining Mara, Harper and Marco's toddler, with cartoons on the TV and some toys.

The rest of the gang from Trident—Ian and Angie Sawyer, Devon and Kristen Sawyer, Jake Donovan, Nick Sawyer, Marco, and Boomer—would be arriving on Friday along with some friends from The Covenant—Mitch Sawyer, Tyler Ellis, and Tori Freyja, Tiny Daultry, and Roxy and Kayla London. Brody and Fancy's next-door neighbors, whose twin five-year-old daughters were going to be flower girls, and her employees from her bakery would be coming as well. Chase Dixon from Blackhawk Security was also attending the wedding and offered to fly everyone west so Fancy and Brody could take this jet today. Meanwhile, a few friends from SEAL Team Four, including Curt Bannerman and his wife Dana, Pete Archer, Steve Romanelli, Neil Radovsky, and others would be flying in from all over the United States. Finally, the Sawyer brothers' parents, Chuck and Marie, US spies T. Carter and Jordyn Alvarez, and Boomer's folks, Rick and Eileen, were arriving on Friday too. The TS Omega Team would be running Trident while the Alpha Team was in Texas for a few days.

At the Evans family ranch on the outskirts of Dallas

people had been busy. Since Fancy's family was scattered around the US, Brody and Fancy had decided to have the wedding in Texas where his large family lived. Every October, his parents threw a huge, old-fashioned hoe-down that all their extended family and friends looked forward to. So many people attended that, as the family had grown, they'd made it a tradition to wear color-coordinated name tags so any newcomers could easily learn who was who, who they were married to, and whose kids were theirs, among other details. It had helped Fancy tremendously when she'd attended her first one a few months ago. Since the family prepared for and ran the annual event with such efficiency, it had been easy for them to organize the backyard wedding—they'd done it before for two of his three sisters and one of his two brothers. Tents, a dance floor, the stage for the band, and catering had all been arranged. Fancy had spent many hours on Skype with her Aunt Denise in Cleveland, and Brody's mom, sisters, and sisters-in-law, planning and coordinating. They'd found a bridal shop in both Tampa and Dallas that stocked the same designers and were able to pick out a dress that all the bridesmaids could order and be fitted for without a hassle. Then there was selecting the right flowers, table linens, band, photographer, videographer, and Lord knew what else. Brody's mom, Elise, had arranged for Fancy's employees to use the kitchen of a local bakery after hours Friday evening to put together and decorate the individualized cake pieces they were baking on Thursday.

Now that he thought about it, Brody realized he hadn't done a tenth of what Fancy and the other women had for the wedding. Oh, he'd helped pick out colors and a few other things, but he knew they'd done so much more. And knowing his family, he was certain it would be an event to remember, even if he hadn't been marrying the woman who'd won his heart.

Picking up her hand, he kissed her knuckles before eyeing the oval diamond surrounded by ruby baguettes set in white gold on her ring finger. It matched the formal collar she was wearing that told the BDSM world she was spoken for. Her wedding band was also white gold, just as his was. They were in his nearby computer bag where he knew he wouldn't misplace the small boxes. He'd give them to Marco, his best man, right before the ceremony.

Brody's fiancée was an incredibly beautiful woman, and he was lucky to have won her heart. Luscious and generous curves, ivory skin with a smattering of freckles on her face, shoulders, and chest, full, gorgeous, auburn hair, and green eyes he could get lost in for hours combined to make most men take an appreciative look. And she was all his—every delicious inch of her.

Fancy smiled at him then reached for her pad and pen. When she sat back up, he noticed she was a little pale and took them from her again. "You're pushing yourself too hard, sweetness. Everything is going to go like clockwork, knowing my family. Why don't you lie down and take a nap for a bit? We have just over an hour before we land."

"But—"

He cut her off. "No buts. Lay down and relax—that's an order. There will be plenty of time to go through your check-list when we get to the ranch. Don't make me spank you." His threat was said in a low, soft tone so Jenn and Alyssa didn't overhear. While they were fully aware of the BDSM club, The Covenant, located in the Trident Security compound, they'd never been in it and didn't need to know what went on behind the closed doors. Alyssa was still a teenager and twenty-one-year-old Jenn didn't want to imagine her surrogate uncles and godfather, Ian, having sex, as she'd told them on numerous occasions. Brody didn't care if Harper or Kat heard him, though, since they were in the lifestyle and knew as well as Fancy did that a spanking could be for a punishment, pleasure, or stress release.

Grabbing a nearby throw pillow, he placed it on his lap and patted it. Sighing, Fancy swung her feet up onto the couch and laid her head on the pillow. "Fine. But when we get to the ranch, I'm sure I'll be running around like a chicken without a head, even with your sisters and mom helping."

Brody ran his fingers up and down her bare arm. "Which is all the more reason for you to sleep now. I don't want you so stressed out that you can't enjoy the wedding . . . and the wedding night," he added with a grin.

———

Fancy climbed out of the SUV Brody had rented at the airport, as Harper parked the one she'd gotten next to it. They'd needed all the space they could get to transport everyone, the luggage, and the bridal party's dresses. It was a beautiful afternoon at Paradise Pastures, the Quarter Horse breeding ranch on 200 acres of land the Evans family owned. In addition to the normal bustling activity on the property, there were vans and people prepping the large area behind the main house where the wedding reception would take place.

The ceremony itself was being held in the one of the ranch's many meadows. It'd been kept clean of the animals for the past six weeks according to Brody's father, Gerard, so no one would be stepping on poop. He'd been seeding and watering the fenced in area, so the grass would be nice and plush. A trellis was being set up and decorated with flowers to serve as the dais where the family's priest, Father Cartwright, would marry the couple. Instead of chairs, bales of hay, covered with soft throw blankets, would be the seats for the guests who'd been encouraged to wear comfortable, western clothing and cowboy boots. Brody would be in his Navy whites for the ceremony before changing into a new pair of jeans and a button-down shirt. As for Fancy's dress, it had a simple, country flair to it, and she'd be able to wear it all day in comfort.

This would be so different from Fancy's formal wedding to her first husband, who'd been killed in a car accident several years ago, with a huge ball gown at a catering hall. But it was perfect for Brody and the woman Fancy had become since meeting him. He'd been the final piece of the puzzle she'd needed to pull her from her grief back into the land of the living, and she loved him with all her heart.

Leaving the luggage in the vehicles for now, she and Brody took out the boxes of pastries they'd brought, then led the way to the front door. Although all the Alpha Team had been to the ranch on many occasions, most of their women hadn't been there before. Harper was pointing out all the animals in the pens and pastures to the east of the main house to Mara who was clapping and babbling with delight. Jenn was telling Alyssa and Kat all she knew about the ranch, having visited several times with her uncles and deceased parents.

Before they reached the door, it swung open and Brody's mom and sister Doreen came out with open arms, hugging everyone they already knew and introducing themselves to the newcomers. Elise gave Fancy an extra-long hug—she'd loved her future daughter-in-law from the moment she'd met her, knowing she was the perfect mate for her son. "I'm so glad you're finally here! I hope you love how we set every-thing up."

"I'm sure I will, Elise. We can't thank you enough for all the work you've put into the wedding."

"Oh, it was my pleasure." She released Fancy and gave her a stern look. "Now, remember what I told you. If there's something you don't like or aren't happy about, I want you to tell me, so we can change it. It's your wedding and you deserve to have it exactly as you want it. I promise I won't be insulted."

"I'm sure everything's perfect. The only thing that would make it not so is if Brody doesn't show up."

The women all laughed as Brody gave her a loving swat on the butt. "Like that would ever happen. You, sweetness, are not going to be the one who got away."

As everyone followed Brody into the house, they cackled like a bunch of hens. There were at least three different conversations going on at the same time, and Fancy found herself trying to follow them all. After dropping the bakery boxes onto the large island in the kitchen, Brody grabbed Fancy's hand and brought her out the backdoor with the rest of the women on their heels. The massive tents were being set up, and there were stacks of chairs and round folding tables waiting to be placed under them. The area had been spruced up for the occasion, and Fancy noted a few new trees and flowering shrubs had been added since last October.

Brody's dad was explaining to the men from the party supply company where he wanted each tent erected but glanced up when the small crowd on the back porch caught his attention. His eyes lit up, and with a few final words to the workers, he strode across the expanse. Brody met Gerard at the bottom of the steps and gave him a hug and some back slaps, which were returned in kind. The older man then climbed the stairs, pulled Fancy into a warm embrace, and kissed her cheek. "Hey, beautiful! It's great to see you. How was the flight?"

"Great. I think the Trident jet has ruined me for commercial travel though."

"I have no doubt," he responded with a chuckle. Letting her go, he grinned at Mara in her mother's arms. "Hey there, sweet pea. You're getting big. Remember me?" The little girl clearly did as she reached out, wanting him to hold her. Without hesitation, Gerard scooped her into his arms. Mara had been fascinated with him for some reason when he, Elise, and Brody's eldest brother, Brett, had flown down to Tampa when Fancy's former brother-in-law had tried to kill Brody during an insane, jealous rage. Corey Maguire had developed a sick obsession with her and had caused the car accident that'd killed his brother and put Fancy into a coma.

He'd gone out of control after Fancy had started dating Brody and had kidnapped his perceived rival and tried to torture him to death—coming very close to succeeding. He'd then been shot and killed during Brody's rescue.

"Fancy, come here." Brody gestured to where he was standing at the gate to the meadow where they'd be saying their vows in a few days. The trellis had already been set in place but was currently bare. The florist would be putting the fresh flowers on it early Saturday morning while the ranch hands arranged the bales of hay for the makeshift pews.

Descending the steps, she joined her fiancé with a smile on her face. "What?"

He pulled her in front of him, facing the trellis, her back to his chest, and wrapped his arms around her waist. She felt him exhale softly against her ear. "That's where I'm going to be standing, waiting for you to meet me so we can become husband and wife. I love you, sweetness, and I plan on telling and showing you that every day for the rest of my life."

———

THE NEXT DAY, WHILE FANCY WAS OUT WITH HIS SISTERS, KAT, Harper, Jenn, and Alyssa, running errands and picking up the last of the bridesmaids' dresses, Brody had gotten together with his brothers, Brett and Brian, to take care of a list of things to do that their father had given him. Gerard and Elise were happily babysitting Mara and a few of their youngest grandchildren who weren't in school yet. Brody's siblings had all taken a few days off work to help get everything ready for the wedding—it was what they did for each other. They were such a close-knit family, willing to drop everything and come running when one of them was in need. He wished Fancy's family was as close, for her sake, but his family was more than willing to make up for what she lacked in that area.

Fancy's parents had never married and had separated when she was little. Her father had then relocated to California where he'd married another woman and started a new family. After that, Fancy's contact with her father had been mostly via phone and emails over the years, with a few, rare visits when his business brought him east. Unfortunately, his wife had resented Fancy and refused to acknowledge her husband's eldest daughter. As a result, Fancy had never met her teenage half sisters. But that was going to change on Friday. After discussing it with Fancy's Aunt Denise, Brody had contacted her father, had a heart-to-heart talk with the older man, and managed to convince him it was not too late to be a part of his daughter's life. It wasn't the first time he'd talked to the man. Brody had called him months earlier to ask permission to marry his daughter, holding onto the traditions and values he'd grown up with. His words must have struck a chord because Glenn Robertson had accepted the invitation Fancy had extended with little hope that it would be acknowledged. She'd been shocked and elated to learn he'd be attending the wedding with his middle daughter, seventeen-year-old Natalie, who'd always wanted to meet Fancy. The youngest sister, Nicole, however, was siding with her mother and refusing to come. But that was all right. Two out of four was better than none.

Brody had also called his future mother-in-law and Fancy's Aunt Denise. The latter was extremely close to her niece, and he'd known it would please them both for her to be included. As for Fancy's mother, Diane Bayles-Wilford, well, she was coming with her third husband. The woman had done her best for Fancy and her brother, Richard Bayles, but working two jobs as they were growing up meant she'd relied on her sister, Denise Bayles, to help raise them. As a result, the siblings usually went to their aunt for advice or help, rather than their own mother, who never really learned how to cope with their everyday problems or, God forbid, a life-altering crisis. Richard also didn't know or care to know how to be there for his family, either. In fact, he'd declined to fly from Hawaii to Texas for his sister's wedding, citing he was too busy with work to attend.

Paying the dry cleaner for his father's dress shirt and pants for the ceremony, Brody grabbed the plastic covered clothing and headed to the parking lot where Brett and Brian were waiting for him in the latter's red pickup truck. He climbed into the rear bench seat and placed the hangers on the hook above the opposite door. "What next?"

Brian put the vehicle in drive and steered toward the exit. "We've got to get the citronella oil for the torches. Dad said we were running low from the last party." When the sun went down on Saturday, thousands of tiny, white Christmas tree lights and dozens of glass-enclosed torches would illuminate the festivities.

While his brother drove, Brody sat back in his seat and glanced around North Dallas where he'd grown up. He liked seeing his old haunts and always had a sense of sadness when he discovered one of them had been sold and renamed or torn down. As they passed his former high school, Brody's cell phone rang. Pulling it from his pocket, he glanced at the screen. Harper. He connected the call. "Hey, Harper, what's up? Don't tell me there's a problem with the bridesmaids' dresses."

"Uh, no." Those two words were spoken in a tone of worry and distraction which immediately had him gripping the phone tighter as he listened. "Brody, Fancy passed out at the dress shop. Suddenly, she got pale and slid to the floor. The paramedics are loading her into the ambulance now. You have to meet us at Medical City Hospital."

"What? Is she okay?" Both brothers spun their heads toward him at his panicked voice.

"I don't know, Brody. By the time the medics got here, she was conscious but disoriented. They think she might be dehydrated. I don't know. We're getting ready to follow the ambulance. Kat's in there with her. Meet us at the ER."

"We're on our way." He hung up and looked at Brian. "Medical City ER, get there fast. Fancy fainted or something and they're transporting her by ambulance."

"Is she okay?"

"I don't know, damn it, just get us there." He hadn't meant to bark, but his stomach was clenched in fear. Try as he might to reassure himself it was a simple case of dehydration and stress, he was terrified something was seriously wrong.

Holding on to the "oh shit" handle above his head as Brian broke a few speed limits and traffic laws on the way, Brody prayed like he'd never prayed before. It felt like the trip took hours, when, in reality, they pulled into the hospital's emergency room parking lot in under fifteen minutes. Brian had barely parked when Brody yanked the door handle and jumped out, running toward the entrance. The automatic doors flew open when he stepped on the black mat in front of them, and he hurried inside with his brothers on his heels. He immediately spotted the women huddled together in a corner of the waiting room.

Harper was the first one to notice him as he rushed over. She held up her hands. "Calm down. She's okay. They started her on IV fluids in the ambulance and she's making more sense now. Kat's still back there with her. They're running some tests, but it looks like it's just stress and dehydration."

His sister Deanna put a hand on his shoulder. "I think it's the same thing that happened when Nana was dehydrated, and her sodium levels got so low it made her all loopy." Brody had almost forgotten about that. His grandmother had been in the hospital for a few days last year and hallucinating until they'd gotten the sodium levels back up. Deanna pointed to a nearby wooden door. "Why don't you go back and talk to the doctor?"

Moments later, he peeked around the curtain to the cubicle he'd been directed to by one of the nurses. Fancy was lying on a gurney, her red hair in sharp contrast to her pale skin and the white sheets. Her eyes were closed, but an EKG monitor was beeping a steady rhythm. She wore an oxygen cannula in her nose and an IV line was in her left arm. Kat stood from the bedside chair she'd been sitting in, gave Brody a hug, and whispered, "She's resting. The doctor will be back in a bit; he's just waiting for the blood results, but he thinks her sodium was too low."

"Yeah, that's what Deanna said. Has she woken up?"

At the sound of his voice, Fancy's eyelids blinked open. "Hi. I'm awake. Sorry about this."

Seeing she was no longer needed, Kat left the two of them alone, heading for the waiting room. Brody grasped Fancy's hand as he sat on the chair, relief seeping into his veins. "Nothing to be sorry about, sweetness. I'm just glad you're okay. How do you feel?"

"Tired. Confused, but that's going away."

"That's good." He gently brushed the hair on her forehead to the side. "Why don't you close your eyes and rest until the doctor comes back?"

"'Kay."

Brody stayed by her side as she slept, ignoring everything else going on outside the cubicle. The only thing that mattered right now was his woman. He was kicking himself for not noticing the toll the stress of planning their wedding had taken on her. But that stopped now. Until she woke up on Saturday morning, put on her wedding dress, and walked down the aisle to meet him, she wasn't going to be allowed to lift a finger or stress over anything. He was certain their family and friends would have no problem finishing all the little details that needed to be taken care of. As of now, Fancy was on bed rest.

He wasn't sure how much time had passed before the curtain was pulled open enough for a gray-haired man dressed in scrubs to enter and yank it shut again. With a clipboard in his left hand, he extended his right. "I'm Dr. Erikson."

Standing and shaking the man's hand, he responded, "Hi, I'm Fancy's fiancé, Brody Evans."

"I understand the wedding is this Saturday. Congratulations."

"Yeah, it is. Thanks."

Fancy's eyes fluttered open and focused on the newcomer. "Hi, Doctor."

"How're you feeling?" He smiled as he leaned against the bed railing.

"Better. Just tired."

"Well, that's perfectly understandable. You've got a lot going on, and I think I'm about to add to it." Brody and Fancy narrowed their eyes in confusion as the man's smile grew wider. "Since you didn't tell me earlier, I'm going to assume you didn't know you're pregnant."

Brody's jaw dropped as fast as his stomach did. His knees went weak, and he couldn't stop himself from plopping down in the chair. While they hadn't exactly been trying to get pregnant, they'd gotten rid of the condoms the night they got engaged months ago. Fancy had gotten pregnant with her first husband but had lost the baby in the car accident that'd killed Patrick Maguire. Her GYN had been optimistic that Fancy would still be able to have children, but there'd always been more than a sliver of doubt in his fiancée's mind. Well, the question of whether she could or couldn't was now answered. *Holy shit. I'm going to be a father!*

Dumbfounded, his gaze met Fancy's and he found her

just as stunned, but then concern appeared on her face. "Doctor, is the—the baby okay? I—"

The man held up a hand, cutting her off. "The rest of your blood levels are good. The sodium is low, as I expected, but not critical. With the IV, it should be back to normal in a little while. Do you have any idea how far along you might be? When was your last period?"

Her head rocked back and forth on the pillow. "I—I don't know. I'd have to check the calendar I keep in my purse. I think Harper has it in the waiting room. My period's always been irregular, and every once in a while, I skip a month, but never more than that."

"Okay. So, four to six weeks, approximately?"

Fancy thought for a moment and said, "No, I'd say six to eight."

"Even better. I'll send you for an ultrasound to confirm everything is fine, which I'm pretty sure it is. Then we'll have a better idea of how far along you are. Once that's done and you're rehydrated, I'll release you on one condition—take care of yourself and don't stress too much over the wedding. It's supposed to be one of the best days of your life, so enjoy it."

Brody stood and shook the man's hand again. "Don't worry, Doc. I'll make sure she relaxes, even if we have to elope."

Grinning, Fancy swatted his arm. "Don't say that. We'll have over two hundred people mad at us."

"I don't care, sweetness. Let them be mad. You and . . . and our . . . *holy shit*." He shook his head in disbelief. "You and our baby are all that matters."

The doctor slapped his shoulder on the way out. "Congratulations. Let me go order the ultrasound."

Turning back to Fancy, Brody just stared at her. She cocked her head to the side. "Are you happy? I mean, we didn't expect this."

"Happy? I'm freaking ecstatic. And I'm trying not to faint 'cause there's not enough room on the cot for both of us." A salacious smile spread across his face. "Well, unless one of us is on top." Leaning down, he brushed his lips across hers. "I love you, Fancy-girl. You've made me the happiest man on Earth. And after we seal the deal on Saturday, we'll start picking out baby names, okay?"

———

STEPPING DOWN FROM THE BACK PORCH OF THE MAIN HOUSE, FANCY followed her seven bridesmaids, two junior bridesmaids, and two flower girls to the gate leading into the pasture. Violin music floated through the air as the wedding guests all turned to watch the group approach. Everything was perfect. Their families and friends had worked hard to make sure everything was just right for their special day. Brody hadn't let her lift a finger since she'd been released from the hospital, telling everyone it was doctor's orders. After their initial shock at her pregnancy, the expecting couple had decided to wait until the reception to announce it to everyone. It'd been hard not to give it away over the past two days.

If anyone had told Fancy three years ago she'd one day overcome her grief about losing Patrick and their baby, she wouldn't have agreed. But time and a special man, who was about to give her his last name, had brought her back to the land of the living. Brody had never made her feel as if her first husband had never existed. In fact, he'd always encouraged her to talk about Patrick and their life together. Most men she knew wouldn't have been confident enough in themselves to accept that a part of her heart would always belong to the deceased man, but not Brody Evans. Her fiancé had told her he was grateful for every day she'd had with Patrick since it had molded her into the woman he'd fallen in love with.

Stopping at the gate, she waited while her Aunt Denise made sure there was a certain amount of spacing between the attendants as they walked down the aisle. Fancy forced herself not to peek around everyone to see Brody. She wanted to wait until she had an unobstructed view of him. Instead, she glanced around at the guests sitting on the rows of hay bales. So many members of his and her families, their individual friends, mutual friends, and co-workers would bear witness to their nuptials. Some of those who couldn't attend had Skyped in their best wishes over the past two days, including the Omega Team, TS West Team, Bea "Mic" Michaels and her team in Scotland, and Jase Atwood and his girlfriend, Brie, in the Caribbean. Meanwhile, Assistant Director of the FBI Larry Keon, King Rajeemh and Queen Azhar of Timasur, along with Princess Tahira and Prince Raj, and several others had phoned to wish the couple well.

She was thrilled to see her father when he arrived yesterday. There had been lots of hugging and tears, with repeated apologies from him for not being a major part of her life before now. He promised that would change, but Fancy knew it would be a struggle for both of them after so much lost time. Her half-sister Natalie had been shy initially, but she quickly warmed up thanks to Jenn, Alyssa, and Brody's teenage nieces and nephews. She even talked about applying to colleges in Florida so she and Fancy could get to know each other better.

In front of Fancy, Harper, the matron of honor, was starting her walk up the aisle. Stepping over, Aunt Denise had tears in her eyes as she said, "You look gorgeous, Fancy. Brody's a lucky man."

And Fancy was the lucky woman he'd fallen in love with. When the music changed to the wedding march, her aunt moved away, and Fancy's gaze went to her very-soon-to-be husband. He looked mouthwatering in his Navy whites standing in front of the flower-covered trellis with his groomsmen lined up next to him. He grinned as he stared lovingly and possessively at her, making her feel like the most beautiful woman on Earth. The ivory, tulle and lace dress she'd chosen had a country flair to it, and her ivory, vintage-style boots complemented it. A friend of Elise's had come earlier to style Fancy's hair into a romantic updo, with bits of baby's breath to complete the look and show off her white gold collar with its diamond and ruby baguettes. While many attendees didn't understand its significance, those who did knew it meant she belonged to Brody long before they'd gotten to this point when they'd make it legal. Today was just the proverbial icing on the cake.

Taking a deep breath, she put one foot in front of the other and slowly approached her future—one that included the little life growing inside her. Through her gaze, Fancy let

Brody see all the love in her heart and felt his in return. When she reached the end of the aisle, he stepped forward, took her hand, and kissed her knuckles, his eyes never leaving hers. "Hey there, sweetness. Fancy meeting you here. You wouldn't happen to be here to marry me, would you?"

Her smile spread, and she gave him a coy look. "Maybe. You might want to hurry, though, before I change my mind."

"Well, then, let's seal the deal and get this show on the road."

HONOR, LOVE, AND CHERISH
JAKE & NICK

Nick Sawyer held up the new butt plug he'd just unwrapped and glared at his sister-in-law Kristen. "Seriously? The Sparkling Unicorn Plug?"

She grinned and toasted him with her margarita. "Because you're one in a million, Nick, so you deserve something unique and special. Besides, I got Jake's approval before I ordered it."

The rest of the women and two men present roared with laughter. A bunch of the submissives from the BDSM club his two older brothers, Ian and Devon, owned had insisted on giving him his own bachelor party, without his fiancé, Jake Donovan, or any other Doms from The Covenant. The group of women included both his sisters-in-law and the wives and girlfriends of his teammates at Trident Security, along with others he'd gotten to know since moving back to Tampa. The two men who'd been invited—Matthew and Sterling—were also submissives at the club. They were both nice guys, although a little too effeminate for Nick's taste—not that he was in the market. Nope, this was his last night as a single guy, and he couldn't be happier. Well, yes, he could. He'd rather be with Jake right now at his bachelor party at his brother's Irish Pub. Thankfully, Nick's party was being hosted in Ian and Angie's apartment at the TS compound and not anywhere public. He would've been mortified opening some of these gifts where people he didn't know could see.

When he and Jake had first gotten together, Nick had no idea he was a sexual submissive. But once Jake had displayed his dominant nature, Nick had been a goner. He'd probably never understand why, but he'd accepted Jake was the only man he'd ever submit to. They'd needed to get past a few obstacles to get where they were now, but there was no place else Nick wanted to be—except, maybe, at Donovan's tonight. It was only at times like these the retired Navy SEAL felt out of his element—he was an alpha male everywhere except in the bedroom—but he was man enough to indulge the women in his life. As long as they stocked the fridge with his beer and not some fruity drink, he was okay.

"Open mine next, Nick!" Kayla London tossed an oblong box into his lap as he sat back in the recliner.

He grinned and shook it. "Knowing you, I'm afraid to." The sassy sub had a wicked sense of humor, so the present was sure to make him groan some more.

After ripping off the wrapping paper, he opened the box and burst out laughing. It was a leather paddle that would leave the word "Mine" temporarily imprinted on his ass when his new husband spanked him with it. Again, the room filled with cackles and giggles as he held up the present and pointed at Kayla. "Thanks. Jake will love it."

The rest of the evening passed by with some funny games, a few shots, and lots of laughs. It was just after midnight when Jake, Ian, and Devon arrived to break up the party. After making sure everyone would be getting home safely, Jake grabbed his fiancé's hand and led him through Ian's Oasis, the grassy expanse between the last two warehouses in the Trident compound. Out of the four oblong buildings, the smallest one had been turned into four apartments—one for each Sawyer brother and the fourth for Ian's goddaughter, Jenn Mullins, who'd been babysitting Kristen and Devon's infant son, JD, for the evening. The entrance to Nick and Jake's and Jenn's apartments was at the rear of the building, with the men's unit being on the second floor.

"Did you have a good time?" Nick asked, following Jake up the stairs.

"Yeah, but it would've been better if you were there."

Jake opened the door and flipped the light switch, so they could see. As soon as the door shut behind Nick, he found himself propelled against it. Jake's mouth slammed onto his, demanding entry. Nick could taste the smooth Jack Daniel's whiskey on his fiancé's tongue as it dueled with his. Grasping the hem of Nick's T-shirt, Jake yanked it up, halting the kiss to pull the garment over his head, and then removed his own. Next, Nick's jeans were unbuttoned, unzipped, and shoved down his legs, his hard-on springing free.

"Hands behind your head, Junior." Jake dropped to his knees. "Not a word out of your mouth, unless I ask you a question, or I'll get a ball gag."

Wide-eyed, Nick followed his Dom's orders. One calloused hand gently cupped his balls while the other stroked his hard cock. Nick's head fell back against the door, his clasped hands sandwiched between them. He bit his bottom lip, fighting the urge to beg for more. His Master would take care of him, but at his own pace.

"Eyes on me, subbie."

Gulping, Nick lowered his gaze. The love he saw in Jake's eyes reflected his own. The man opened his mouth, and Nick's cock disappeared inside. A low groan vibrated in Nick's throat as Jake's tongue swirled around him before he took him deep. Nick gasped when Jake swallowed around the tip of his cock. His Dom knew how much the sub wanted to pull his hands free and take control, but he wouldn't. What Jake would give him as a reward for his submissiveness and obedience was far better than anything Nick had experienced in his life. The anticipation heightened his senses, and in the end, his orgasm would be explosive—he knew from experience.

Jake pulled off him. "Who's your Master?" His tongue lashed across the tip of Nick's cock.

"You are, Sir."

"Who do you submit to?" Another lash.

"You, Sir."

"Whose name will you take tomorrow?" Another.

"Yours, Sir."

"Who is going to honor, love, and cherish you for the rest of your life?"

Jake's hands gripped Nick's hips as he gazed up at his

fiancé. There was no doubt what the answer would be. "You, Sir."

"Damn straight, Junior."

That hot mouth closed around Nick's shaft again, and this time, Jake didn't hold back. His head bobbed up and down as he gave Nick the blowjob of a lifetime. Hollowing his cheeks, he sucked hard before laving the hard flesh from root to tip. He rolled Nick's balls in one hand. Reaching up with his other, he held out two fingers in a silent order. Nick spit on them, knowing exactly where they were going next. The hand snaked up between his legs and the fingers delved between his ass cheeks, finding his tight hole. Nick's knees shook as Jake worked his most sensitive body parts into a frenzy. One, then two of Jake's fingers breached Nick's sphincter, and he almost cried out at the delicious sensations bombarding him. His balls drew up tight, his vision going hazy. His breath was coming in short pants. He was close, so close, but he knew he had to wait for permission. Pleasing his Dom was more important to him than finding his own pleasure.

"Come for me, Junior. Come in my mouth. Give it all to me."

Yes!

As soon as Jake's lips formed a seal, and he sucked hard, Nick detonated. His eyes slammed shut. Fireworks flashed behind his lids as streams of cum shot from his cock into his lover's mouth. Jake swallowed every drop until Nick was fully spent and sagged against the door, trying to catch his breath.

With a final lick, Jake looked up and grinned. "Relax,

babe. Let's get you to bed, so I can fuck your fine ass, then get some sleep. We've got a big day tomorrow."

———

With Nick by his side, Jake strode from the parking lot to the dock leading to the party yacht they'd rented for the wedding. In their naval dress whites, both men were garnering appreciative glances from men *and* women along the way.

It was a beautiful day for their wedding—the sun was shining, and a nice breeze was blowing in from the gulf. With the warm weather, though, neither man wanted to stay in uniform after the ceremony, so Nick was carrying a garment bag with more comfortable clothing for them.

At the end of the long dock, several guests, including Nick's folks and Jake's mother, were already gathered, waiting for the couple to arrive.

Even though Jake's sub belonged to him in every sense of the word, today they'd make it legal. He hadn't realized until they'd gotten engaged how much that would mean to him. Until he'd fallen hard for Nick, Jake had thought he'd spend the rest of his life either going from one short-term relationship to another or completely alone. He definitely hadn't thought he'd fall for his teammates' younger brother. But fate had other plans and had sent him the most incredible man to love, and Jake would never forsake the gift he'd been given.

"Oh, good, you're here. The flowers, photographer, videographer, and DJ are here, and Fancy's staff just brought the cake inside, but the judge hasn't arrived. Did you call her yesterday to remind her to be on time?"

Rolling his eyes, Jake kissed his mother on the cheek, then shook hands with her new boyfriend, Chad Walker, a former NYPD detective. "Don't worry, Mom. She'll be here—it's still early. Half the guests aren't even here yet, and we have about thirty minutes 'til we shove off."

The two men greeted the rest of their loved ones who'd already gathered, including their teammates and their wives—Ian and Angie, Devon and Kristen, Brody and Fancy, Marco and Harper, and Boomer and Kat. The photographer Emma Donovan had hired stood nearby and took candid shots of everyone. They were lucky—even in this day and age, not every gay or lesbian couple had the full support of all their family and friends. If Jake's father were still alive, they would have had to face that reality. The man had been a bigoted bastard in the first degree. Jake shook off the painful memories before they could fully form—they were in the past, where they belonged. His future stood right next to him, laughing and smiling. Nick was his sunshine, the man who'd pulled Jake from the darkness and showed him how to let go of the things he couldn't change.

More guests arrived as they boarded the yacht. They'd kept the list small—sixty people who meant the most to them. While a few couldn't make it, including friends from California, where the couple had lived together for a year and a half, almost everyone had accepted the invitations even though they'd been given short notice.

In the main cabin's dining room, Jake's brother, Mike, and his girlfriend, Charlotte, aka Mistress China, were going over the last-minute food and drink details with the event manager. While Jake and Nick had wanted to keep things simple, Emma had overridden them. She'd been in her element, organizing everything in the scant two-week time period they'd given her. Mike, Charlotte, all the Trident women, and a few club members had stepped up to help her, while the engaged couple had been in Miami, working on a case they'd easily wrapped up in time for their nuptials. Emma had contacted Nick's mom, Marie Sawyer, several times to consult with her before his parents had flown in from North Carolina a few days ago.

Those onboard already included Alyssa Wagner, a teenage girl Jake and Nick had saved from an abusive father, her guardians and Boomer's parents, Eileen and Rick Michaelson, Shelby and Parker Christiansen, Roxy and Kayla London, and several others. Nick's cousin Mitch Sawyer, who co-owned and ran The Covenant, and his submissives, Tyler and Tori, had also arrived a few minutes ago.

A hand slapped down on Jake's shoulder as he watched several dolphins frolicking in the water. "Hey, pretty boy."

Grinning, he turned and gave T. Carter a man hug. "Glad you could make it. Wasn't too sure you would. Hey, Jordyn." He kissed Carter's submissive girlfriend on the cheek. The couple were two of the most covert US spies on the planet, yet their friendship with the men of Trident ran deep. Carter hadn't missed a wedding among them yet, although he'd cut it awfully close a few times.

"Hi, Jake." The petite woman ran a hand down his arm. "Damn, you and Nick are smokin' in your dress whites. Can

Carter borrow them some night? I think I have another fantasy that has to be fulfilled."

As her Dom frowned, Jake chuckled, knowing that would never happen. Although he didn't know a lot about Carter's background, including his first name, he did know the man had done a brief but redacted stint in the Marines back in his teens.

"Come up with another fantasy, Jordy, because I'm never dressing up like pretty boy here."

"You'd never be able to do him justice." Nick slid in next to Jake, then shook hands with Carter and kissed Jordyn hello. "Glad you could make it."

"We wouldn't miss this for the world," Carter said with a grin. "Another I'm-never-getting-married Trident boy is going down hard—pun intended."

Laughter filled the air, and once again, Jake was glad Nick had talked him out of eloping. Having their family and friends with them as they tied the knot was the right thing to do.

By the time they were scheduled to launch from the dock and head out into the Gulf, all the guests and the justice of the peace had arrived, much to Emma's relief. Judge Lily Bradshaw was a Domme at The Covenant and had cheerfully agreed to perform the nuptials. The only loved ones missing were six-month-old JD and two-year-old Mara, Marco and Harper's daughter, who were at Kristen and Devon's apartment with two club submissives who'd volunteered to babysit, so their parents could enjoy themselves.

As they cruised across the calm waters, the guests took their seats where the ceremony would take place at the aft of the boat. To soft music, Jenn walked down the short aisle, dressed in a blue sundress and holding a small bouquet of flowers. Jake and Nick had forgone the traditional best man and asked Jenn, who was a surrogate niece to the men at Trident, to be their maid of honor, carrying the wedding rings for them. Once she reached where the judge stood, Nick escorted Marie down the aisle, followed by Jake and Emma.

Finally, the time had come—the two men stood facing each other in front of everyone. As Judge Bradshaw gave an inspirational invocation before the vows, Jake's gaze never left Nick's. His heart swelled within his chest. The love he had for this man would never be matched. They'd been made for each other, and Jake knew that to his dying day, he'd love no other as he did Nick.

"Do you, Jake, take Nick to be your lawful husband, to honor, love, and cherish all the days of your life?"

He wiped away a tear that threatened to fall. "I do."

"And do you, Nick, take Jake to be your lawful husband, to honor, love, and cherish all the days of your life?"

"I do. Hooyah!"

Jake grinned as the guests and the judge laughed. *Brat.*

"The rings, please?"

Jenn handed the two platinum rings to the judge who then held them for the men to take.

"Jake, you're first. Place the ring on Nick's finger and repeat after me. With this ring, I thee wed."

Jake slid the symbol of his love onto his sub's hand. "This is the first and last time I'll say these words, Junior. With this ring, I thee wed."

It was Nick's turn to wipe away an emotional tear. Out of

the corner of his eye, Jake could see both mothers, Nick's dad, Chuck, and several other guests were doing the same.

Nick blew out a deep, shuddering breath as he placed the ring on Jake's finger and then repeated the same words. "With this ring, I thee wed."

"By the power vested in me by the state of Florida, I now pronounce you husband and husband. You may kiss your groom."

Cupping Nick's jaw in his hands, Jake wasted no time kissing him as his husband for the first time as the guests cheered for them. He even managed to get a few swipes of his tongue in, a little reminder of what was to come when they were finally alone later.

Grabbing Nick's hand, Jake held it high as they turned to walk down the aisle. Behind them, the judge announced, "It's my honor to introduce to you Jake and Nick Donovan."

———

The reception was in full swing, with everyone having a grand time, when Jake and Nick found themselves surrounded by Ian, Devon, their teammates, Brody, Marco, and Boomer, and Chuck Sawyer. Not that it made a difference to Jake, but his new father-in-law was a self-made, real estate billionaire. Something that'd come in handy when Ian and Dev had gone into the private sector and used their trust funds for the startup money.

The Sawyer patriarch slapped Jake on the shoulder. "Welcome to the family, son. Although you've been part of it for a long time—this just makes it legal."

"Thanks, Chuck."

"Your brothers and I have a few things to discuss with you two. Consider them wedding presents." Pulling an envelope out of the back pocket of his dress pants, the older man handed it to Nick.

The newlywed couple had matching, confused expressions on their faces as Nick opened the envelope and began to read, with Jake looking over his shoulder. Nick was the first to realize what he was seeing. "Holy shit."

Yeah, that was putting it mildly. After Chuck had made his first few million, he'd set up the trust funds for his sons, which had been garnering interest ever since. Upon graduation from high school, each brother began to receive a small, monthly stipend, as long as they did either a four-year stint in the military or got a bachelor's degree in college, then continued to work for a living. When Ian and Devon had each hit the age of thirty, they'd been given full control over their accounts. At twenty-seven, Nick still had a few more years to get his. But, today, Chuck had handed him the paperwork that voided the initial directives he'd stipulated when setting up the trust funds. Nick now had full access to his money to do with as he pleased.

"Dad . . ." Nick shook his head in disbelief. "I—we didn't expect this. Thank you."

"You're welcome, boys." He gave Nick, then Jake, a fatherly hug. "You both deserve it. Your mothers and I are very proud of both of you. Never forget that."

Ian cleared his throat, catching their attention. In his hands were several more envelopes. He handed the first one to Jake, another to Nick, then the rest to Brody, Marco, and Boomer, all of whom furrowed their brows.

"What's this?" Brody asked, opening his.

"This," Ian responded, "is the paperwork that gives you each a share of Trident Security."

Several sets of eyes went wide, but it was Boomer who voiced what they were all thinking. "What? Are you shitting us?"

"You're my favorite turds—I'd never shit you." Chuckles spread through the mostly-stunned group.

Devon rolled his eyes and took over. "But, seriously, we knew once Nick joined us, we'd be putting his name on the company letterhead. Then it occurred to us, without you four, Trident Security probably wouldn't exist. You supported us when we first thought of going private, then gave up a lot to come work for us, not knowing if it would be a success. Blood related or not, you're our brothers and, now, co-owners of Trident."

"Of course, Dev and I still have the controlling shares—that's a given."

Still dumbfounded, Jake held out his hand to Ian. "You didn't have to do this. I don't know how to thank you."

"Sure you do. Make sure Junior's junk stays hidden from my view and we're even." Barks of laughter filled the air as Ian shook Jake's hand.

"Done."

BURNING EMBERS
JENN & DOUG

"So, how's the internship going?"

Twenty-two-year-old Jenn Mullins grinned at the woman who'd taken over her waitressing position at Donovan's Pub about two months ago. Although Daniella Mavis was eleven years older than Jenn, the two women had bonded after being held hostage during an attempted robbery at the restaurant after it'd closed following a party for Jenn.

Sitting at the bar next to the waitress station, Jenn swallowed a sip of her soda before answering. "It's going great! I love working in Kayla's office. She's so nice and always takes the time to explain things to me. Her clients love her too."

Social worker Kayla London and her pediatrician wife, Roxy, were friends of Jenn's uncles, and Kayla had been a huge inspiration for Jenn to choose social work for her intended career. She had one more semester to go before graduating early from the University of Tampa with her bachelor's degree in sociology. Then, she'd start on her master's in social work. The opportunity for Jenn to intern at Kayla's office had come up, and she'd jumped at the chance.

"Are you working with just her?"

"Oh, no. There are seven other social workers in her office. Most of them are nice, but honestly, I think one or two need to retire. They just don't seem to be into their jobs anymore, you know what I mean?"

Daniella smiled as she placed her lunch-time customers' drinks on her tray. Monday tended to be a slow day at the restaurant—only three tables were currently taken. A few regulars sat at the bar, but the bartender, Missy, took their food orders on top of handling their drinks. "I know what you mean. If they were doctors, their bedside manners would suck, right?"

"Exactly!" She popped a French fry in her mouth from her almost-finished lunch, then noticed her friend frown at something over Jenn's shoulder. "What's wrong?"

Without waiting for an answer, Jenn glanced over her right shoulder, and her stomach and heart both sank as her mouth went dry. *Damn it.*

Sighing, Daniella picked up her tray. Before she left the bar to deliver the drinks, she quietly said, "Sorry, Jenn."

Sorry, indeed. The last person Jenn had expected to see walk into Donovan's on a Monday afternoon was Doug Henderson. And she certainly hadn't expected to see him having lunch with another woman. Not that Jenn was his woman, though she wanted to be. She'd been in love with the man for the past several years, but he didn't even know she existed. Actually, that wasn't true. He knew she existed —he'd been her bodyguard twice in the past. The first time was when her father's, godfather's, and surrogate uncles' jobs as US Navy SEALs had come back to bite them all on the ass. The other time was when her Aunt Angie's friend's DEA job had resulted in a threat to everyone associated with Trident Security. Doug had even taken a bullet in the chest for Jenn, and his partner had been killed, before she'd been kidnapped and then held hostage along with Angie. Now recovered, Doug was in charge of Trident Security's Personal Protection Division, working for her godfather, Ian Sawyer, his brother, Devon, and with their teammates, who were newly appointed co-owners of the private security business that had numerous government contracts.

The trouble with all that was the fact that Doug still saw her as the teenage girl he'd been assigned to protect, not the grown woman she'd become since then. It probably didn't help her situation that he was thirty years old. She didn't have a problem with their age difference, but, apparently, he did. And now he was here, having lunch with a disgustingly pretty woman who was closer to his age. Jenn hated the brunette on sight and wanted to crawl into a hole in the ground, so she didn't have to see them sitting in one of the booths across the room.

At least her lunch hour was almost up—she had to get back to the office. She usually ate there or grabbed something nearby with Kayla or the other two interns but had changed things up for today after she'd been chatting with Daniella on the phone last night. It hadn't taken much pleading on the other woman's part for Jenn to promise to stop in for lunch to see her and the other employees she'd worked with. Talk about lousy fucking timing. Daniella knew

Jenn was in love with Doug and had been supportive when the younger woman bitched whenever Doug had treated her like a child.

She studied him in the mirror for a moment. He was wearing a pale yellow polo shirt with the TS logo on the right side of his chest, black cargo pants, and black rubber-soled shoes. He was just as muscular as Jenn's uncles were, though it'd taken him a while to build his strength back up after being shot just over two years ago. His dark-brown hair was shorter than it'd been the other day when she'd seen him walking into the TS offices. She didn't need to see his eyes to remember how they were only a shade lighter than his hair.

After throwing enough money on the bar to cover her tab, she silently waved goodbye to Daniella as she entered the kitchen to drop off an order, and then to Missy, who was busy with her own customers. Pulling her sunglasses out of her purse, she put them on, then hurried to the front door, hoping Doug was too distracted to notice her. There was no way Jenn wanted him to introduce her to the woman he was with.

She'd just pushed open the inside door when she heard Doug's deep, rumbling voice. "Hey, Jenn!"

Pretending she hadn't heard him, she continued into the small vestibule, letting the door close behind her while pushing open the outside one. With any luck, he wouldn't come after her. He didn't have a reason too, and that increased her disappointment as she strode across the parking lot toward her car.

As she approached her Ford Edge and pushed the button on her key fob that unlocked it, a black Cadillac SUV pulled into the spot next to it. The front doors opened and two men in their early twenties climbed out.

The driver was on Jenn's side, and he eyed her up and down. "Well, hello there, sweet thing. I'm Chaz. What's your name?"

She rolled her eyes as his friend came around the front of the vehicle and joined his buddy. Both had tattoos and piercings and were wearing baggy jeans and expensive sneakers. The passenger wore a T-shirt, while the driver sported a tank top. Jenn was certain they belonged to one of the gangs that tried to rule parts of the city. But right now, they were blocking her driver's door. "It doesn't matter what my name is because I'm in a hurry and you'll probably never see me again. Now, if you'll excuse me." She gestured to her vehicle.

Instead of moving out of the way, the driver leaned against her SUV. "Well, that's a shame, since I really want to see you again, sweetheart. Tell me your name and phone number, and maybe I'll let you drive away."

For the first time since she started working at the county's social services office, Jenn regretted their strict rule that no firearms were allowed in the building because she usually had one in her purse. Her uncles had trained her to shoot the SIG Sauer P238 her godfather had gotten for her on her twenty-first birthday, along with a concealed-carry permit, and she'd become a damn good shot. Not that she'd pull out a gun just because these two assholes wanted to mess with her, but she'd feel more secure if she had it with her. But it wasn't the only weapon her uncles had trained her to use. She had pepper spray on her, a pocket-sized Taser, and in the inside of the driver's door, if she ever got it open, there was an expandable baton that she was supposed to use on an attacker's balls, throat, and knees, in that order. In the back seat was a baseball bat. In her hand, she held her key fob with the key to her apartment between her index and middle finger. Although she'd been taught how to shoot and defend herself in any situation, since she'd been old enough to do so, her uncles had stepped up that training and drilled it into her after her first hostage situation. Her aunts had been going through similar training as well. But as much Jenn practiced shooting and close quarter defense, she still got nervous when she was alone and facing a potential threat.

They were in broad daylight, in a nice part of the city though, so she really didn't think she'd need any of those weapons. She just had to stand her ground and show these idiots she wasn't intimidated by them and they should back off, right? She hoped so. Jenn really didn't want to cause a scene, but if they didn't get out of her way, she was going to be late getting back to the office. *Shit.*

––––––––

"Hɪ, Doᴜɢ."

He smiled at the pretty, brunette woman standing outside Donovan's pub, waiting for him. This was their second date, and the only reason he'd agreed to meet Lynette Johnson at this particular restaurant was because it was unlikely he'd run into Jenn now that she no longer worked there. His bosses' niece had a serious crush on him, and he tried to discourage her as much as he could, without being rude about it. He didn't want to hurt her, but having just turned twenty-two not too long ago, she was far too young for him—plus her uncles would kill him if he made the slightest of passes at her. Jenn was a beautiful woman, but she needed someone her own age, who wasn't so jaded about life in general.

As a retired Marine, with three rough tours in the Middle East under his belt, and a private-security bodyguard, Doug had seen far too much bloodshed—some of it his own—to date someone as young and innocent as Jenn. At least Lynette could relate to him—she'd done two tours in Afghanistan while in the Army and was now a patrol officer on Tampa PD. Her friend and co-worker, Dakota Swift, had introduced her to Doug, after insisting the two would get along great due to their similar backgrounds and personalities. Dakota's boyfriend, Logan "Cowboy" Reese, a retired Marine Raider, was an operative for the same company Doug worked for. After a casual introduction at a local cop bar last week, Doug had asked Lynette out on a dinner date which had gone well on Saturday. He hadn't been swept off his feet by the woman, but he found her attractive and liked her enough to try to get to know her better. They'd had a nice time talking about the military, their careers, and other things over dinner. Dakota had been right—they did have a lot in common.

"Hey. Hope you weren't waiting long." He'd gotten a phone call right before he'd left the office, so he'd been running a few minutes late. Lynette had the day off from work, but Doug was only on his lunch hour.

"Nope. I literally pulled in about two minutes ago. I was just about to text you to let you know I was here."

He opened the outside door to the restaurant, and gestured for her to precede him, before following her through. He then held open the inner door for her as well. He was glad she was in front of him because she didn't see him falter when the beautiful blonde sitting at the bar caught his attention. She wasn't facing him, but he'd recognize her profile anywhere.

Shit. Of all fucking days for Jenn to come here for lunch. Doug should've come up with a different place to meet when Lynette had suggested Donovan's, since it was near her condo and not far from his job at the TS compound, but it was too late to change things now. Maybe Jenn wouldn't notice him if he sat facing the front of the restaurant.

Trying to keep his gaze from straying back to Jenn, he followed Lynette to a booth on the other side of the room from the bar. Unfortunately, she was a cop, so she had the same instincts he did. She took the bench that would have her facing most of the large room. Anyone trained in defense tactics knew to keep their backs to the wall as much as possible. Since a threat would most likely come from the main entrance, the best place to sit in here was with one's back to the kitchen door and pray a threat wouldn't come from there.

Any other time, it wouldn't have really bothered Doug, because Lynette was carrying just like he was, but as he sat in the other side of the booth, he hoped Jenn wouldn't notice him. It wasn't that he didn't want to see her, it was that he shouldn't want to see her. The young, blonde woman had him thinking things he shouldn't, yearning for things he couldn't have, at least, not with her.

"So, how's your day going?" Lynette asked as she got comfortable and they waited for Daniella, the daytime waitress who'd taken Jenn's position, to bring them lunch menus.

"Good, I guess." As he proceeded to fill her in with some mundane stuff that he'd dealt with that morning, out of the corner of his eye, he noticed Jenn stand, put her sunglasses on, then walk quickly toward the door. Her back was stiff, and he got the impression she was upset about something. His gaze followed her as she hurried to the door, and he found himself interrupting his conversation to call out to her as she reached the exit. "Hey, Jenn!"

Apparently, she hadn't heard him, since she didn't even pause before leaving the restaurant. Doug turned back to face Lynette who was looking at him curiously. He apologized, trying to act like nothing was wrong. "Sorry. That was Jenn, my boss's goddaughter—she lives at the Trident compound. Just wanted to say hi and introduce her to you."

Yeah, that was a lie. The last thing he wanted to do was introduce Jenn to the woman he was currently dating.

Lynette smiled. "Oh, so that's Jenn. Dakota's mentioned her a few times. She goes to U of T, right?"

"Uh, yeah. She's getting her bachelor's degree in sociology, then going for her master's in social work." For some stupid reason, he'd been about to tell her more about Jenn, but thankfully, Daniella came by and handed them menus. "Hi, Daniella. Thanks." Against his better judgment, he added, "Is Jenn okay? She ran out of here pretty quickly."

The waitress glanced toward the front door, then back at him with what seemed to be a forced smile. "Oh, she's fine.

Her lunch hour is almost up, and she had to hurry back to work."

Doug had a feeling Daniella wasn't being entirely truthful, but he let it slide. There wasn't anything he could do for Jenn now that she'd left, and he really needed to focus his attention on his date. "What would you like to drink, Lynette?"

"A ginger ale would be great."

He nodded at Daniella. "Make that two."

"Great." She jotted the order on the pad she was holding. "I'll be right back."

Before she had a chance to go to the bar to get their drinks, a man at a table by the front window called out to her. "Miss, can we get the check please?"

As the waitress made her way to her other customers, Lynette and Doug opened their menus and studied their options. Since he knew the main menu by heart, Doug eyed the specials for the day. A tingling sensation at the back of his neck had him glancing around, and he noticed Daniella staring out the front, plate-glass window, frowning. Something was clearly wrong, and Doug immediately felt it involved Jenn.

Standing, he said to Lynette, "I'll be right back."

Not waiting for a response, he strode purposely toward the front door that Daniella was also heading toward. He stopped her before she could open the heavy, wooden door. "What's wrong?"

"I think two guys are harassing Jenn out there."

"Stay here, I'll take care of it."

Again, not waiting for an answer, he strode out, pushing

both doors open. Spotting Jenn and her vehicle, Doug zeroed in on the two dickheads blocking her from getting into her SUV. Even with her back to him, he could tell from her body language these weren't friends of hers. *Oh, hell no.*

Doug jogged across the lot, slowing as he came up behind Jenn. Her hand was in her purse, and he wondered if she was holding the gun, Taser, or pepper spray he knew she carried in there. "Jenn? Everything okay?"

She glanced over her shoulder at him, and he saw relief in her eyes. Before she could answer him, the bigger of the two assholes, the one wearing a white wife-beater, asked, "So, that's your name, huh? Jenn? Nice."

"Leave the lady alone and take a hike," Doug warned, his tone low and threatening. Taking Jenn by the upper arm, he pulled her behind him.

"Fuck off, man, we're talking to her. This ain't none of your business."

"See, that's where you're wrong. This is my business. And if you know what's good for you, you'll get lost."

Pushing off Jenn's car, the guy pulled out a switchblade. His buddy followed suit. *Well, fuck.*

Doug took a step back, giving himself room to defend himself. He didn't pull the concealed 9mm from its holster at the small of his back because there were pedestrians, adults and children, walking through the lot—oblivious to or ignoring the situation going on in their midst. If he fired, any of them could get hit, or the bullet could go even farther, striking someone driving by. Besides, these assholes needed a beating, and Doug was more than happy to give it to them. "Jenn, go back inside."

"No—"

"Inside, Jenn! Now!"

Sneering, the guy in the wife-beater stepped forward with the knife pointed at Doug. "Don't listen to him, *Jenn*. Derek and me are going to make hamburger out of him, then you and us are gonna have some fun." With that, he lunged forward.

———

TERROR COURSED THROUGH JENN AS DOUG AVOIDED THE SWINGING blade. There was no way she could leave him alone with these two jerks attacking him. With her hand on her mini Taser, she tried to pull it out of her hobo bag, but the guy named Derek pushed her out of his way, and she fell to her knees. Her bag landed next to her, and most of the contents spilled out. Derek kicked at all of it, getting it out of his way as he looked for a way to ambush Doug, who waited for his chance to disarm the asshole named Chaz. So far, he'd only been able to thwart the attempts to stab him.

He glanced her way. "Jenn! Get the fuck out of here! Go!"

She knew Doug could defend himself against one of them without any problem, but with both swinging knives at him, who knew what could happen. Her gaze darted across the asphalt, searching for her pepper spray or Taser. The spray container was under the Cadillac, and the Taser was nowhere in sight.

Jenn had two options—run back to the restaurant for help or do what her uncles had trained her to do. Jumping to her feet, she rushed to the driver's door of her SUV and threw it open. After grabbing the retractable baton from the inside pocket, she flicked her wrist, expanding it to its full length. Raising it above her head, she brought the weapon down hard onto Derek's forearm. The asshole screamed in pain and dropped the knife, but Jenn didn't stop there. She couldn't go for his balls or throat because he was now bent at the waist, holding his arm. Instead, she reared back and swung for his knee. The loud crack was immediately followed by an agonized howl, and he collapsed to the ground.

In the meantime, Derek's scream had distracted Chaz just long enough for Doug to land a right cross on his jaw, stunning him, then grab his assailant's wrist that was still holding the knife and twist it until the weapon fell harmlessly. Doug yanked Chaz's arm behind him and shoved him against the rear of the Cadillac.

The sound of running feet caught Jenn's attention, and she looked up to see Doug's date hurrying toward them. She stopped a few feet away and took in the scene. Derek was moaning in pain on the ground, while Chaz was cursing at Doug, who just pulled the guy's arm higher on his back, eliciting some begging. Doug then patted him down for other weapons—finding none.

Once he was done, the other woman handed Doug a pair of handcuffs, causing Jenn to wonder why she had them in the first place. She then retrieved both knives before making sure Derek didn't have any others on him either. "Patrol is on their way. Next time, Doug, tell me something's going down instead of leaving me sitting there." Nodding at the baton Jenn was still holding, the woman grinned. "Sounds like you broke a few bones. Good for you. I'm Lynette Johnson. You're Jenn, right?"

Startled and shaking, now that things were under control, Jenn just nodded. Lynette took the baton from her and placed all three weapons on the hood of Jenn's vehicle. "I work with Dakota Swift. She's mentioned you a few times."

Well, that explained the handcuffs but not how Lynette knew who Jenn was. However, right now, Jenn couldn't care less. She turned to Doug, who was scanning her from head to toe—anger and concern mixed in his eyes. "Are you okay?" When she nodded, his expression became thunderous. "What the fuck, Jenn? I told you to go back inside! You could have gotten hurt or killed, for fuck's sake!"

She narrowed her eyes at him. "But I didn't, did I?"

"No, she didn't. In fact, she did a damn good job of disarming this idiot."

Having Lynette stand up for her had Jenn feeling even better, until a thought crossed her mind. "Oh, no. Don't tell my uncles. They'll want to kill them and hide the bodies. Please don't tell them."

Lynette chuckled. "From what I've heard about Ian Sawyer and his team, that's a very good possibility. But, unfortunately, they're probably going to hear about it." She paused to flag down two patrol cars that flew into the parking lot with their lights flashing and the last of their sirens fading away. She then pointed to Derek. "First, these two are going to the hospital for X-rays. I'm pretty sure you broke his arm and possibly his knee. His buddy will need to be checked out too. Then, they're both heading to booking, followed by the city lockup after their arraignments.

"The arresting officers will need both your statements to file the charges. You'll probably need to testify at the grand jury hearing too. I'm sure we'll be able to charge them with a few felonies. The point of all that was your uncles will find out within twenty-four hours at the latest. They have too many friends on the force *not* to hear what happened."

"Shit," Jenn murmured. When Doug glared at her, she rolled her eyes. "After the last ten minutes, Doug, I think I'm entitled to curse, so don't tell me not to. I'm an adult, remember?"

He didn't respond, but she could see his jaw tighten as he handed Chaz over to one of the police officers before giving another a rundown of what had happened.

"Jenn!"

She turned, and Daniella threw her arms around her. "Oh my God! Are you okay?"

Exhaling a heavy breath, she sagged into her friend's arms, disappointed they weren't Doug's.

———

Six hours later, Jenn sank into the couch in the living room of her apartment. She was finally alone—well, except for Beau, TS's first trained protection dog, who'd followed her from Ian's apartment and had jumped up and laid down next to her. The dog always seemed to know when his humans needed him. Jenn buried her face into his furry neck and let the tears, which she'd been holding back for hours, finally flow. She knew it was from an adrenaline crash—she'd experienced it more than once before—but she hadn't wanted

Doug to see her cry. He already thought she was still a child, and that would have proven it to him.

Officer Johnson—Lynette—had accurately described what would happen after the police had transported the two suspects to the hospital. The only discrepancy had been Derek had needed surgery on his knee—Jenn had broken his patella, much to the delight of her aunts.

After calling Kayla and filling her in on what had happened, and that she needed the rest of the day off to give her statement to the police, Jenn had called her godfather. Lynette and Doug had convinced her it was best that she be the one to tell him. Before the scene had been cleared, her uncles—Ian, Devon, Brody, Marco, Boomer, and Jake—and Jake's husband Nick had sped into the parking lot and jumped out of their vehicles, desperate to see for themselves that she was unharmed.

Brody had retrieved the surveillance footage from Donovan's outside cameras he'd installed a few years ago. The owner of Donovan's, Mike, was Jake's brother. After playing it for everyone to see, and congratulating Jenn on kicking ass, Brody had made a copy for the cops to put into evidence. While Boomer had taken Jenn's vehicle back to the TS compound, Ian had driven her to the police station with Doug following. Her godfather had stayed with her throughout the ordeal of repeating her story several times, then signing a statement attesting to the facts. Chaz had been arraigned and transported to the city jail until his next hearing. Meanwhile, Derek was under guard at the hospital and would be arraigned when he woke up from surgery.

Once Ian, Jenn, and Doug had arrived back at the TS

compound, everyone there had wanted to hear their versions of what had happened, instead of relying on the second-hand info they'd already received. After all the hubbub had died down, Angie had invited Jenn and Doug to eat dinner with her and Ian, but both had declined. Doug had claimed he had work to finish, and Jenn had thanked Angie but told her she wasn't hungry, which had been the truth.

For a twenty-two-year-old, Jenn had gone through a lot of emotional trauma—hell, it had only been in the last few years—but today, she'd proven to her uncles, and herself, that her training had paid off. She just wished Doug was convinced she could defend herself if needed. While she was grateful he'd shown up when he had, he was still pissed she hadn't followed his orders to run away. Her uncles were annoyed about that too, but at least they'd all said they were proud of her.

Beau tensed and let out a low growl. Moments later, there was a knock on the door. Whoever it was, the dog must have sensed they weren't a threat—not that one could easily get near her apartment—and he relaxed again, his tail thumping on the couch.

Figuring it was one of her aunts or uncles checking up on her, Jenn wiped her eyes with the back of her hands, then stood and answered the door. Her heart rate sped up when she found Doug standing there in the small foyer she shared with Nick and Jake, who had the apartment above her. The burning embers, smoldering in her core, flared at the sight of him. There was no way what she felt for this man was fabricated in her mind. She just had to convince him of that fact.

He frowned when he saw her red eyes. "You've been crying. Are you okay?"

She shrugged. It wouldn't do her any good to deny her earlier tears. "Yeah, just an adrenaline crash. I'm fine." When he just stood there, staring at her, she asked, "What are you doing here?"

Doug suddenly seemed unsure of himself. "I—um—I was getting ready to head home and just wanted to make sure you're okay."

"I'm fine," she repeated, doubting he believed her. "Do you want to come in?"

He glanced over her shoulder into the apartment, then shook his head. "I—um—better not."

Damn, the man frustrated her. "Why? Because we'd be alone, and you think I'm going to jump you?"

"Jenn—"

She crossed her arms and glared at him. "Don't 'Jenn' me, Doug. I get it. You think I'm too young for you and I'll always be that way. Well, you know what? You're wrong. Look at my Uncle Devon and Aunt Kristen—she's twenty-nine and he's thirty-nine. And Jake's nine years older than Nick. And Uncle Brody is six years older than Fancy. So you being eight years older than me is not a big thing—at least, not for me or anyone else."

"They may have big age differences, but they're all a lot older than you, Jenn. And it's not just the age thing. You've got this—this hero complex thing when it comes to me—"

"What? Are you kidding me? Trust me, Doug. What I feel for you has nothing to do with you being my bodyguard and taking a bullet for me. Do you know how scared I was while

Aunt Angie and I were being held hostage? I was scared more for you than myself—I thought you were dead or dying, and there was nothing I could do about it. If you'd died, I would've been devastated. Not only because I would have lost you, but because I would never have the opportunity to tell you I love you." *Oh, shit. I did not just say that!*

The stunned look on Doug's face told her she'd, indeed, just confessed her love for him. Again, he shook his head. "Jenn—"

Before he could say anything else, she threw caution to the wind and her arms around his neck. Her lips met his, and Jenn almost melted. For years, she dreamed about what it would be like to kiss Doug Henderson, and here she was doing it.

Doug froze as she brushed their lips together, then his hands grasped her hips. When he tried to push her away, she tightened her hold around his neck. She wanted something to remember if this was the only time she ever kissed him. She wanted him to kiss her back and prove to her this wasn't a one-sided attraction she felt between them.

Parting her lips, she slid her tongue between them and licked his mouth. His hold on her hips increased, but instead of pushing her away, he pulled her closer. *Oh, God!* He was hard—for her. Doug groaned, then suddenly, he took control of the kiss. One hand came up and grabbed her hair. He angled her head to the side as his tongue plunged into her mouth, dueling with her own.

The kiss was better than she'd dreamed it would be— and she'd dreamed of it often. Jenn ran her fingers through his hair and rubbed her chest against his. Her nipples pebbled and sent delicious sensations down to her clit. It throbbed, wanting more. Doug pivoted them and pressed her against the door jamb. Jenn moaned when she felt his erection thicken between them. Heaven—she was in heaven and never wanted to leave.

Without warning, Doug ripped his mouth from hers and practically jumped out the door into the small foyer, panting. "Shit! Jenn . . . that—that shouldn't have happened. I shouldn't have—"

Tears welled when she saw the horror he felt reflected in his eyes. That, more than anything, tore her heart out. "Don't say that. I kissed you, Doug. I wanted to, and I wanted you to kiss me back. I've wanted it for so long. Don't stand there and tell me you don't feel the attraction between us. You wouldn't have kissed me like that if you didn't. You—"

"Jenn, stop." He ran a hand down his face. "I'm sorry, but it shouldn't have happened, and it won't happen again. I'm sorry."

"It will if you get over yourself and let it. Goodbye, Doug." After slamming the door in his face, Jenn turned her back to it then leaned against it. Sagging to the floor, she shook her head. "Shit."

Sawyer Family

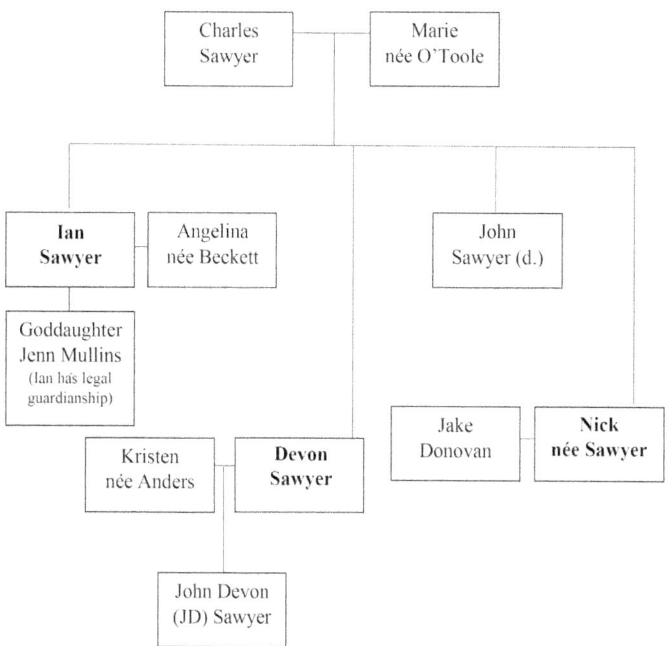

Boomer Michaelson's Family

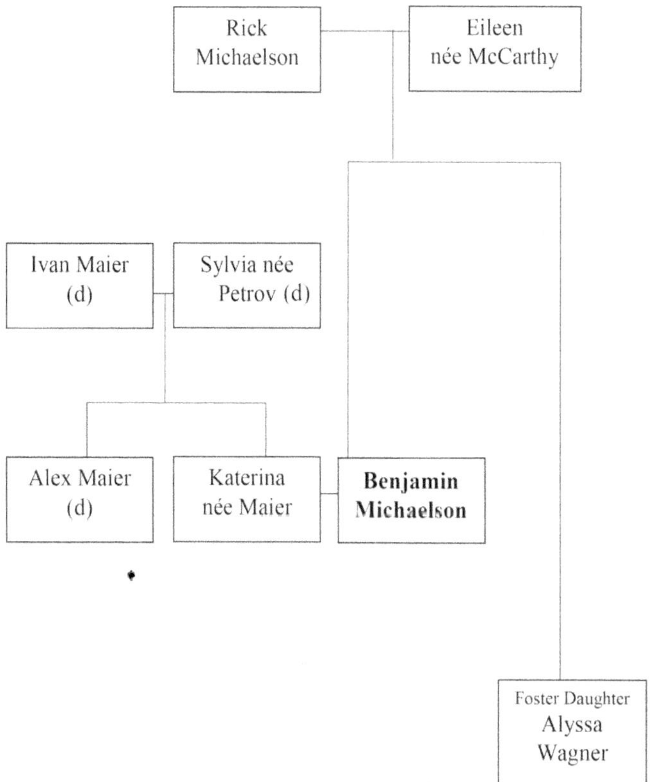

Jake Donovan's Family

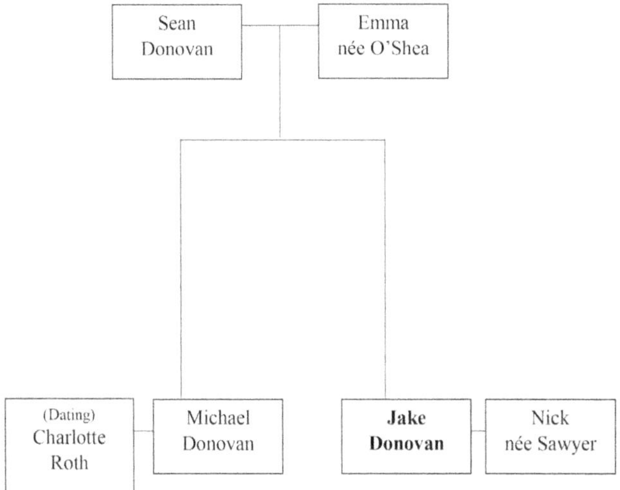

Marco DeAngelis's Family

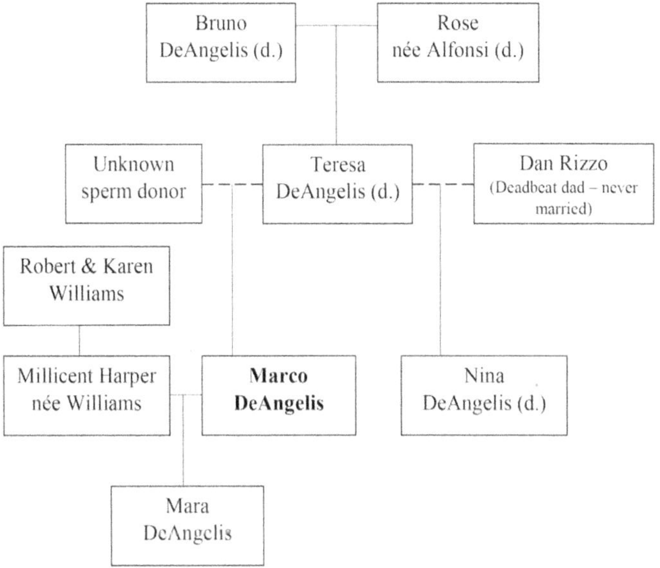

Brody Evans's Family
(Minus nieces and nephews)

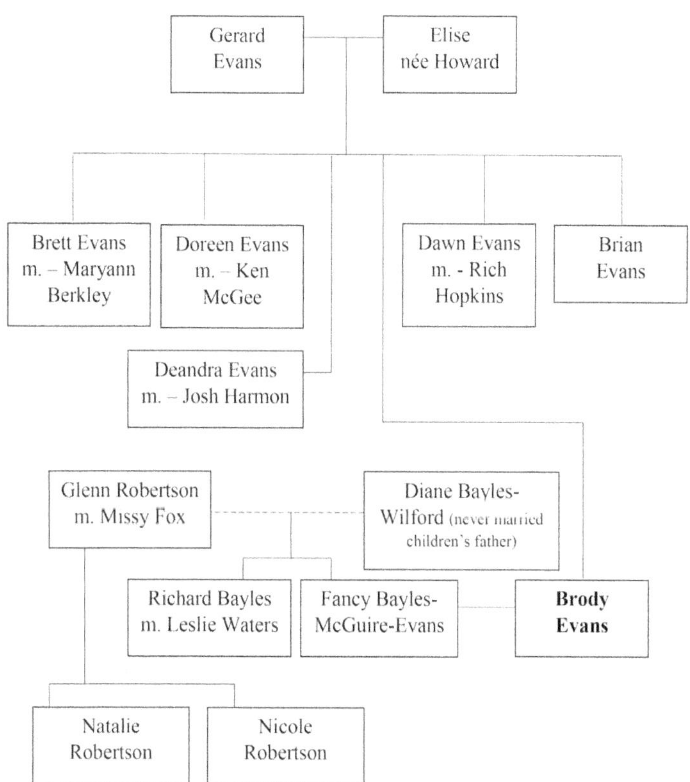

I hope you've enjoyed the Trident Security Field Manual. It was a blast to write, and I found myself laughing and shedding a few tears during the process. Please consider taking a moment to post a review—they are always appreciated.

If you're following the best reading order of the Trident Security series and its spinoff series (which is available on my website), then up next is *Forty Days & One Knight: TS Omega Team Book 2.*

For the best reading order, check out the printable list on my website - www.samanthacolebooks.com/pages/best-reading-order.

Want to know what's coming next? Join my Facebook Group -

Samantha Cole's Sexy Six-Pack's Sirens...

Or sign up for my newsletter -
samanthacolebooks.com/mailing-list

OTHER BOOKS BY SAMANTHA COLE

***Denotes titles/series that are only available on select digital sites. Paperbacks and audiobooks are available on most book sites.

THE TRIDENT SECURITY SERIES

Leather & Lace

His Angel

Waiting For Him

Not Negotiable

Topping The Alpha (MM)

Watching From the Shadows

Whiskey Tribute

Tickle His Fancy

No Way in Hell: A Steel Corp/Trident Security Crossover (co-authored with J.B. Havens)

Absolving His Sins

Option Number Three (MMF)

Salvaging His Soul

Trident Security Field Manual

Torn In Half

Burning For Him

***HEELS, RHYMES, & NURSERY CRIMES SERIES

(WITH 13 OTHER AUTHORS)

Jack Be Nimble: A Trident Security-Related Short Story

*****The Deimos Series**

Handling Haven: Special Forces: Operation Alpha

Cheating the Devil: Special Forces: Operation Alpha

The Trident Security Omega Team Series

Mountain of Evil

A Dead Man's Pulse

Forty Days & One Knight

The Doms of The Covenant Series

Double Down & Dirty (MFM)

Entertaining Distraction

Knot a Chance

Finding His Forever (MM)

Reclaiming His Soulmate

The Blackhawk Security Series

Tuff Enough

Blood Bound

Master Key Series

Master Key Resort

Master Cordell

Hazard Falls Series

Don't Fight It (MMF)

Don't Shoot the Messenger (MFM)

Don't Burn Bridges

THE MALONE BROTHERS SERIES

Her Secret

Her Sleuth

Her Savior

LARGO RIDGE SERIES

Cold Feet

***ANTELOPE ROCK SERIES
(CO-AUTHORED WITH J.B. HAVENS)

Wannabe in Wyoming

Wistful in Wyoming (M/M)

COCK & BULL SERIES (M/M)

Scout

Rico

STANDALONES

Where the Broken Bloom

Scattered Moments in Time: A Collection of Short Stories & More

Sweet Revenge

The Sugarplum Fairy (M/M)

***THE BID ON LOVE SERIES
(WITH 7 OTHER AUTHORS!)

Going, Going, Gone: Book 2

*****The Collective: Season Two**

(with 7 other authors!)

Angst: Book 7 (M/M)

Special Collections

Trident Security Series: Volume I

Trident Security Series: Volume II

Trident Security Series: Volume III

Trident Security Series: Volume IV

Trident Security Series: Volume V

Trident Security Series: Volume VI

ABOUT SAMANTHA COLE

USA Today Bestselling Author Samantha Cole is a retired police officer and paramedic who now writes heart-pounding romance in multiple forms—MF, MM, and ménage. From military heroes to rugged cowboys and small-town heat, her stories blend passion, loyalty, and danger in perfect balance.

Awards:

Wannabe in Wyoming (co-authored by J.B. Havens) won the bronze medal in the 2021 Readers' Favorite Awards in the General Romance category.

Scattered Moments in Time won the gold medal in the 2020 Readers' Favorite Awards in the Fiction Anthology category.

Where the Broken Bloom (formerly *The Road to Solace*) won the silver medal in the 2017 Readers' Favorite Awards in the Contemporary Romance category.

Sexy Six-Pack's Sirens Group on Facebook
Website: www.samanthacolebooks.com
Newsletter: samanthacolebooks.com/mailing-list

facebook.com/SamanthaColeAuthor

instagram.com/samanthacoleauthor

bookbub.com/profile/samantha-a-cole

goodreads.com/SamanthaCole

amazon.com/Samantha-A-Cole/e/B00X53K3X8

tiktok.com/@samanthacoleauthor

youtube.com/@SamanthaACole-bp6yu